BLUES FOR A DEAD LOVER

by

CHARLES NUETZEL

WRITING AS "JOHN DAVIDSON"

The Borgo Press
An Imprint of Wildside Press

MMVII

Dedicated to
My wife

Brigitte

SECOND EDITION

Contents

Introduction 5

Chapter One 9
Chapter Two 19
Chapter Three 28
Chapter Four 39
Chapter Five 50
Chapter Six 59
Chapter Seven 70
Chapter Eight 81
Chapter Nine 95
Chapter Ten 109
Chapter Eleven 117
Chapter Twelve 130
Chapter Thirteen 144
Chapter Fourteen 154
Chapter Fifteen 163

About the Author 175

Introduction

Blues for a Dead Lover was written early in my career, and based on a nightmare idea!

It all started when I was engaged to my future wife, and she returned to Germany to visit her family. It was our first real separation. What if she never returned? After all, marrying me would mean living in America, isolated from her family. It was a serious move. What if she decided to stay there, and never come back to me?

That haunted me. I ended up considering it a great concept for a book. Well a germ, anyway.

Just shows you the evil twist of a writer's mind. Even nightmares turn into story ideas. Heck, writers use every sense and awareness and experience as basic food to mentally digest into story plotlines.

Well, back to the nightmare.

What if Brigitte never returned to America?

Of course, said my ego, it wouldn't be because she didn't want to? So, of course, she would want to return.

But: what if it was beyond her control? What if…what?

Well. She might be killed! Why not consider that kind of nightmare possibility?

Are there no limits to the imagination? No

shame? Apparently I'd rather have her dead than happily somewhere else in the arms of another man!

Yes. Come to think of it. I suppose that was my attitude. Better dead than thrilling to another lover's touch!

Horrid thought, that!

I needed to write a book about it all. Get the bitter images out of my mind! And so I did, somewhat scrambled and changed and all that. Naturally. I wasn't about to create real-life events, I wasn't interested in offering up some kind of bio-material to the vast public at large.

But in re-reading the book I realized I had used some real-life touches in the story. Brigitte was there in the opening passages; there are elements of real-life events. But, of course, hidden within the story background.

I had devised a leading character who was not a writer but a jazz musician.

I focused the question in my mind: what does a person do when they lose the most important thing in their life?

This, of course, was the theme of the story.

Then I offered up the background and setting: a story of a man's journey through hell to happiness set on a stage of show business and Las Vegas in the '60s. This was the town of the Sands and the Clan and the big swingers. Glamour USA!

Next came the details:

Bill Carter's life was the world of jazz, blowing a trumpet, and his career was blooming, and soon he'd be married. Everything looked wonderful, at last.

Then the accident happened, and his life was

crushed, and career and everything else went down the tubes in a rush to escape the pain.

It is also the story of his rediscovery of love, and how he ended up rebuilding his life.

To me this is a story based on a romantic notion and a nightmare, and a sense that life does, and must, go on in its own fashion to bring about the healing process. Life is full of blues for lost loves, for lost people, for lost elements that were and remain so very important to our living experience.

—CHARLES NUETZEL
Thousand Oaks, California
August 2006

Chapter One

Bill Carter pulled the trumpet from his lips and stepped to the mike, looking into the dimness of the audience surrounding the bandstand. His eyes flicked across to the table where Laura was sitting.

"Ladies and Gents, the next number is *Laura* for my woman Laura."

He placed the horn to his mouth, and the first silken notes floated out over the audience as the four other musicians took up the accompaniment.

People gathered on the dance floor and started swaying to the slow ballad. It was the last number of the evening, and Bill milked it for a good seven minutes. When the last mellow note faded from the air he stood back, and let his eyes drift to Laura as she sat staring starry-eyed at him.

If only she didn't have to leave the next day for New York, he thought bitterly, laying down his trumpet and briefly glancing at the men in the combo.

"See you around!" he told Don Jenson, the bass man, an old friend.

"Say, don't forget the party tonight."

"How could I?" he smiled, stepping off the band stand and moving to the small, two-foot circle the

9

club owners called a table, where Laura was sitting.

"You were wonderful as usual," she greeted, extending her hands out to his. They squeezed their fingers together and then he sat down next to her. "Only trouble, we can't dance together to that wonderful music!"

He laughed and then sighed, tired. He didn't say anything for a long while, then he finally blurted out: "It's a damn thing you going!"

"Hush! Let's not talk about it, now!" she whispered. "Let's make this evening perfect. As if it were the very last. We should always live our lives for the moment, as if there is no tomorrow."

"Ah, but there's always tomorrow!" He gazed into her eyes, never wanting to stop attempting to reach her very soul in such a manner. The love they shared seemed as if it had existed forever, and would continue on throughout time itself, for they were soul mates.

"All the tomorrows are now, and now is forever," she murmured. "I love you."

Just then a heavyset man stepped up, his lips clamped around a thick cigar. He pulled a chair to the table and said: "Hi, there, sweethearts."

"Can't you leave a guy alone with his girl?" Bill asked half seriously.

"You'll have plenty of time, later tonight!" the man observed, a roguish grin on his face and a twinkle in his eyes.

"For an agent you know too damn much!" Bill laughed, finally pulling his eyes away from Laura's and looking at the man who had placed them into the club and was arranging a few big deals for the group.

"I talked to Larson today," Hanson said, seriously. "He's interested in looking you over for a recording date. He'll be here tomorrow, so blow up a storm."

"Progressive or—"

"Both. He has two labels and if he doesn't like the swinging of one style, he's sure to like the other. Who knows, maybe he'll record you on both..."

"You've done a lot for us, Hanson!"

"Think nothing of it!" the man exclaimed. "Have connections, and after a little string pulling people jump! Plus I get my percentage!"

Bill had heard about the man's connections, and it was rumored that they included the Syndicate operations, but that really didn't matter. The so-called Syndicate ruled Las Vegas, and if they could get a feature spot there, it might help a lot. But it would have to be a feature in some show, not the lounge bit, since they'd been through that before and it didn't gross anything but money. Which was fine, only Bill wanted more. The bigger his reputation, the better his chances in the future. The music business was a tough place to make a living, even for a short time, but for the long haul, it took a lot more than a flash or some gigs here and there across the country. Even Vegas could be limited to mere flash—fast money, little fame. Or it could make a big name for a few lucky professionals. This kind of advance man, agent, promotional push, could make the difference. Hanson stood and then after saying goodbye, he left.

Bill turned his attention to Laura, again. She was smiling at him. "You've really come along way haven't you?" she asked.

11

"From a kid in the slums to a feature sideman in some of the top bands in the country—I guess so. And it was a long haul for the trio, now combo. We did a lot of dinner dates, weddings, private parties, stuff that barely paid the bills." He paused and then added: "Only thing is, I've always wanted to make the point on my own. My own group, you know."

"Sure," she nodded.

"And to think it's all happening so fast. And at the right time. Just when I'm going to get married. You must be my good luck charm!" he exclaimed, excitedly.

"That all? Just a lucky charm to wear around your horn?" She laughed at the private joke.

"You're more than that. Without you I don't think I'd ever want to blow a note again. It's all for you, now. You've changed my life, totally turned me around from a driven man to a man with a realistic dream."

"Don't ever give up your dream, Bill. Never do that."

"I don't have to. I have you."

"Even so, you have a God-given talent!"

"And that's being in love with you. That's been God's real gift to me."

"And you're my personal gift from God," she murmured, leaning closer. "When you play *Laura* to me, it really is like being made love to. Maybe even better."

"Better?" he moaned in mocked pain. "I thought I was the best."

"Well, the way you blow that horn, well it's the best I've ever experienced." She giggled at that.

"Sometimes I wonder about you. You have such

a…naughty mind."

"Oh, come on, I'm a pure virginal type, a lady."

"Not from what I've discovered," he grinned. "Hardly a virgin."

"I'm pure, anyway." She giggled. "And, well, they say a woman should be a lady in the living room, and in the bedroom she's supposed to be a wild—"

He shook his head, finger touching her lips, stopping the words. "You are too pure to say whore!"

She simply smiled.

That was the last thing they said to each other for a long time before the club was closed down to the public. They just sat there, holding hands and gazing into each other's eyes. There was a lot to see in Laura's eyes; all the love and pride that a woman feels about the man she wants, desires, and is about to marry. She was going to make one hell of a wife.

"Say," a voice interrupted their spell, "What're you doing?"

It was Terry Anson, the girl that sang with the group on weekends. And under other circumstances she'd be fun to enjoy after a late night gig. She was nicely stacked and always wore a low-cut gown meant to attract a man's eyes.

The woman was gazing down at Bill as if wanting to climb onto his lap. She was an outright flirt, but one that followed through when the man called her bluff.

"What do you think?" Laura asked, in a rather cool voice. "Making plans for the wedding, when I get back."

Terry flashed her a sharp look, then said: "Oh,

that's right. You're going to be gone for a while. Leaving our Billy-boy all alone. Now don't you worry about anything? We'll take care of him. He won't be lonely."

"He better be. Late at night, anyway," Laura stated, matter-of-factly.

"Oh, honey, I wouldn't think of stepping into territory that isn't free for all to farm."

"Not what I heard," Laura stated.

"Well, believe me. I've never been with a married man, if that's what you mean," Terry pointed out quite seriously. "Until they're legally hooked…"

"Well, do me a favor and considered this one wrapped up in a package with a name-tag, *Laura's Private Property.*"

"Nobody owns another person," Terry observed.

"No. I suppose not. But…"

"Hey, girls," Bill broke into the quick exchange, "remember, I love ya both."

"But not," Terry observed, sweetly, "in quite the same way. I respect that."

"You better," Laura announced, this time a little lighter. "Or I'll be back to scratch your—"

"Now, now," Bill scolded in a mocked voice of alarm.

"Her vocal cords, honey, nothing more!" Laura announced with a laugh, but a very seriously possessive look in her eyes.

It was Terry who offered the closer with: "I couldn't be happier for Bill. He's lucky to have you. And, quite honestly, I'd never consider touching another woman's man…and that's what he is. Flirt though I am. And he's one hell of a guy. If only…but he's taken, I know that."

"You better know it!" Laura offered meaning-fully. "Mine forever and a day, then for the rest of eternity."

"Branded in the brain?" Terry offered. "You are a wonder."

"No. Just a girl in love with her man."

"Who loves her back," Bill offered, gazing sweetly into her eyes.

Terry shrugged and moved off, bouncy breasts and all. "Be right back…need a quick drink!"

Laura watched the other woman, saying: "I think she has the hots for you."

"And every man in slacks."

"Or skirts, maybe. But I think she's more than just hot for you, Bill. Don't let her get too serious about it."

"I won't." He considered that for a moment, then shrugged it off. "She's an outrageous flirt. That's all."

"And the men just love a woman like that!" Laura observed. "She's very popular. But…"

"But what?"

"Nothing really. I actually like her, as long as she just flirts with you in a kidding way, that's okay. If I thought it was serious I'd not leave tomorrow."

"Oh, *God*, Laura. I have a terrible secret to tell you!"

She frowned, almost frightened by the tone of his voice.

"Terry is *very* serious about climbing into bed with me. You best call off your trip and stay here and protect me from her passionately lustful charms. What man could turn her down?"

She laughed at that, relieved sounding.

15

"Please, save me from her. Stay here, forget your New York trip! Please!"

"Oh, I think you're safe enough. If I can't trust you now, how will I ever be able to trust you in the years to come?" She tenderly touched his cheek. "I just really think it is nice you have a tempting woman around who is hot for you...kinda an acid test. If you can survive the *Temptation of Terry* then I'm safe for a life-time. Lucky me!"

They both laughed at that, each comfortable in their mutual love to not really consider the other woman as any kind of threat.

Terry obviously was taken by him. And her flirtations suggested an open offer to share a bed, but she wasn't pushing it. Until he was married, apparently, she figured all bets were off. But it was all, really, a good-natured kind of near innocent flirtation. As long as he didn't step over the line, Terry was not about to push the matter, other than making it obvious she was his for the taking.

Don Jenson stepped up, with Terry in hand, and grinned. "Well, how about a round of drinks! For the travelin' lady."

She laughed knowingly, countering with: "Don't try flattering a girl. I know better. Any excuse for a party!"

He shrugged, good-naturedly, offered: "Heck, we can't let the big man's girl go off without a drink to her happiness and speedy return! Party time or not!"

Laura smiled up at him and Bill turned and said half bitterly: "Two months! That's the *speedy* return?"

"Look at that!" Terry laughed, lightly. "Plays

16

around all his life and then meets some gal and can't be split with her for a few months."

The humor in Terry's voice had a hidden bite to it that wasn't missed by the others.

"I'm sorry," she finally said.

"Forget it!" Bill told her, turning his attention back to Laura. They stared at one another, then he glanced at Don. "You guys be a bunch of pals and blow a few dance tunes for us. We never get a chance to dance..."

It took three minutes to organize the small combo again and by that time the manager of the club had sent a round of drinks for the small party group.

As Bill and Laura stood and danced, Terry sat, glaring at the two of them. Her mouth was almost a thin line and her eyes sad.

But Bill only noticed her once as he turned in her direction, then he forgot all about the young woman. She was beautiful enough, and maybe if Laura hadn't come along he might have had an affair with Terry. Now such an idea was out the window. He had the only woman he would ever want; there would never be another Laura.

The gentle feel of her body moving against his was exciting. He wanted to take her in his arms and carry her into some bedchamber where they could be left alone for the rest of the night. But it was impossible for him to walk out on his friends who had arranged the small party. After thirty minutes or so it would be different; but he had to make some attempt to slow things down so they could leave.

It wasn't for an hour before they got away. Not until after three or four rounds of strong whiskey.

By the time they were in his car, heading toward his apartment, they were both slightly high and laughing at anything. But that was one thing about Laura, she could laugh at the drop of a feather. She was a sport and one hell of a lot of fun. A girl who had never given herself to a man before; and even though Bill had never been one to seduce virgins, it had been different with Laura. Much different. Something wonderful and perfect and beautiful.

They were in love.

Chapter Two

They had been in the apartment for over an hour before he once again brought up her leaving the next day. He'd been holding back the bitterness of it as long as he could and the liquor finally worked down all resistance.

The room was dark around them, only lighted by a small candle in the far corner, on which Laura had romantically insisted. They were stretched out on the bed, lying still, yet their eyes were looking at each other. A light of deep sadness was on Bill's face as he looked down at her perfect form.

"I don't know what I'm going to do when you leave, Laura," he told her.

"Don't look so sad, darling!" Laura demanded, smiling. "Come on down here to me, you lover boy."

He kissed her lips, eagerly. She returned the kiss not only with her tongue but with her whole body.

Then they started making love, seriously. He kissed her throat and moved down to the swell of her breasts. She trembled under him. Her hands caressed his back, gently at first and then urging him harder, pulling his head deeper and deeper into the fullness of her, until finally they couldn't stand the torture any longer and anxiously united in frantic ecstasy, until their bodies were soothed with the exhaustion.

For a long time they lay there, half asleep, then finally he felt her stir and sit up.

"You know, Billy-boy, I think I could use a drink, now!" she laughed, brightly.

The rest of the night was filled with small talk, lover's talk, and plans for their future together, plans for their marriage when she returned. Then they made love once more; blending their bodies together in the caresses and kisses and actions of love until exhaustion covered them with a dreamless sleep.

The next morning Bill Carter took her to the airport, both of them lost in their own thoughts. He kept struggling to keep from sharing a lot of bitter frustration and pain at her leaving

The drive was for the most part in silence. Depression was heavy in the air. He knew that this was the last time he would be seeing Laura for several weeks, and even though he realized how silly it was for him to be so broken-up, he couldn't help himself. There was a tightness in his throat that he couldn't get rid of.

"This is silly!" he finally told her, as he directed the car into the parking lot outside the International Airport.

"What?" she asked.

"Oh you'll only be gone for a little while...yet it seems like it will be forever. If anything ever happened to you..."

"Don't be silly!" she told him, reaching out and patting his arm affectionately.

20

"I know. But—that's the point. What would I have done if I'd never met you?" he sighed, bringing the car to a stop into a small parking space.

"Probably banging it with Terry or somebody like her, from all I've learned about your past life of sin."

He shrugged that off, almost annoyed by the words. "You're all that matters!"

She laughed nervously. "You act as if you won't see me again. As if something terrible was going to happen! I'm here, right now. And that's all any of us ever have, right now."

He gulped at the hardness in his throat. "Now who's being silly," he managed. Then he sobered, getting control of his emotions. "We better get going. We don't have much time and I want to have a couple of cocktails with you before you leave."

"I double that!" she laughed, moving away from him. They both got out of the car and he pulled her baggage from the back seat. Then they started for the huge building several hundred feet away

It took twenty minutes to take care of everything, getting the baggage checked and her seat number assigned, and then finally they settled in the cocktail lounge, ordered martinis, and held hands over the table, just gazing at each other like two school kids.

The martinis came and he raised his in a toast:

"To a quick return."

Then he downed half of his drink.

She sipped hers.

"It's going to be lonely," he told her.

"Why? Just keep yourself busy. Your agent said that there might be a recording contract offered to you this evening. You'll be so taken up with it all that you won't have time to think about me." A crafty look came into her large brown eyes. Then she teased with: "And if Terry Anson has anything to say about it you won't be too lonely."

"Laura!" he scolded, seriously. "You know me better than that."

"You can ignore Terry?" she countered, teasingly. "Really?"

"Well, what can I say? I told you don't go and save me from her temptations."

"Oh, sure. Best that you pass all the tests before the wedding night."

"I'm not that kind of man, and you know it." He reached out, as if to get her in his arms, even though the table was between them.

"Flight 705 to New York boarding at Gate 9," came from the speaker over the bar.

"That's it!" she said in a sad voice.

Hurriedly Bill paid for the cocktails and then the two of them stood and walked out. It only took them a few minutes to get to Gate 9 and they walked all the way, hand in hand, not saying anything.

"I think I better go, now!" Laura said when they arrived in front of the gate, turning toward Bill. "I don't like long goodbyes."

She lifted her lips to his and then they kissed each other lightly, her form melting one last time to his before she stepped away and then moved through the gate.

He wanted to shout to her not to leave, to come back and not go. But he just stood there watching her walk toward the huge, four-engine jet.

He didn't leave until the plane had started to taxi

down toward the airstrip, then finally, choking down the hardness in his throat, he moved back along the walkway toward the bar. He needed some drinks. There was a helpless and terrible feeling inside him that he would never see her again. He couldn't get that undercurrent out of his mind. He kept telling himself it was foolishness; imagination. But it felt too damned real. The only way to numb it was with a drink. Liquor would dull the feeling; all feeling.

Half an hour later he stepped from the bar, after two quick martinis. He was pretty high and the fearful pain dulled.

As he climbed into his car and started the engine, he wondered what in the world could have made him fear that he wouldn't be seeing Laura again. It had all been silly. He'd been feeling sorry for himself. Things would be dulled without her around. But, after all, she'd be back in a short enough time and then they would be together for the rest of their lives.

She was the first woman he had ever really fallen for in a serious way. The others were only one night stands. He'd enjoyed the swinging scene, musically and socially. Women had always been there when he wanted one. But his whole life was dedicated to music—right out of high school into college where he studied hard to get his degree in music. Later, after college, there had been a series of jobs with name bands. Then in the army for a two year stretch which became one swinging ball after another. He'd ended up as a staff musician, playing shows for the other poor slobs who hadn't been as lucky as himself. He'd met Don Jenson, and the two of them were back to civilian life at the same time.

A few gigs with small groups followed and he later organized his own trio with Don. As to women, they were always there. If Terry had been around then, she would have added her body to the list of so many others who had passed through all the beds he'd rented on one night stands. In his world it had never seemed possible that a prolonged love affair could blossom into anything meaningful. Women were there to share night-lunches in the wee hours, devoured and forgotten.

That was the trouble with him. He'd been spoiled by having it his way. Laura, though, was different. She was the real thing. And strong-willed. Now the love of his life was off doing her thing in New York. He hated that. He was just spoiled rotten.

It took only twenty speeding minutes to get back to the apartment that he had shared with Laura for the last two weeks.

His head was spinning by now and he had a large day ahead of him that afternoon.

But there were several hours left to sleep off the booze.

He slept!

He was aware of floating, at first, then suddenly he realized he was swimming. Where, he didn't know.

Laura was in the water next to him, splashing and laughing. "Come on I'll race you to shore!" she shouted and started kicking out in the direction of the sandy beach several yards away, not waiting for Bill to take up the challenge.

Reluctantly he started after her, keeping slightly behind so that he could watch her moving in the wa-

24

ter.

Finally she sprang to her feet and ran for the shore. He rushed after her and lunged as she touched sand. Quickly he grabbed her feet and pulled them out from under her.

After a moment of breathing hard he groped up alongside Laura and ran his hand along her figure, up to the roundness of her breasts.

She didn't move.

"Hey what's wrong?" he cried, laughing and sliding up so that he could see her face.

She stared up blindly at him, not moving, not breathing, not living.

She was dead!

He screamed, horrified. Then choking sobs broke from his mouth.

"You can't die. I need you. I have to have you!" he yelled, grabbing hold of her and bringing her into his arms.

But she didn't respond, just lay there limp and dead.

"How'd you die? How'd you die!" he demanded, closing his eyes to hold back the bitter tears.

He opened his eyes and she was gone. In her place was Terry Anson, her body naked and pulsing with life.

He gasped, terror filling his lungs.

"Where's Laura!" he demanded, sliding desperately away from her. "Where's Laura!"

"Oh, you don't want her! I want you!"

He screamed and got to his feet and ran down the beach. He ran until his lungs hurt and he thought he was about to die.

25

Then suddenly he saw a figure in the distance. He rushed toward it as he made out the lovely features of Laura. She was standing there, her arms outstretched, waiting for him.

He rushed into her arms, sobbing. "Why'd you do that? Why? Why?"

"Oh, don't be silly!" she told him. "I'll be back in a short time. You'll get along. Just keep busy!"

He stared at her in surprise because she was standing at the airport, saying goodbye to him, like she had that morning. She smiled and waved her hand and then rushed toward the plane.

He ran after her, crying for her to come back. But she only laughed and told him not to be silly that she would be back in a little while.

Suddenly Bill was sitting up in bed, looking at the far wall and trying to shake aside the realism of that horrible dream. But for a long time he couldn't do it.

Finally he slid out of bed and started dressing. He had to keep himself busy. The emotional reaction he was having, because of Laura leaving him, was more than just a little frightening. There wasn't any reason for it.

For a moment he had the vague idea that maybe he'd been working too hard the past weeks. Then the strain of knowing that Laura was leaving for a while had drained into another part of his inner being.

If something happened to her, he'd simply shrivel up and stop existing.

But that didn't make sense.

That dream. And the feeling that had been plaguing him for days, now. It had to be over work!

It just had to be.

Taking a deep breath he decided that he needed a drink. Something to relax his raw nerves.

A nervous laugh broke from his lips. Maybe it was just stage fright. Maybe just because of the record deal that might be opened that evening.

He decided that was what it was, and walked out of his room, down to the lobby of the hotel and into the cocktail lounge.

Chapter Three

There wasn't anybody around the club except a few clean up maids and the four musicians in Bill Carter's combo. The others had gotten here about fifteen minutes before and were running through a new arrangement that Don had made for the group.

Bill sat and watched for a while, trying to keep the throb of his hangover down to a degree where he could ignore it.

Finally Don turned and looked at him.

"What you think of it?" he asked, stepping down from the stage and walking over to Bill. "It's empty without you but I guess you can figure out what can be done from your end."

Bill nodded. "It'll do. Want to try it out tonight?"

"Sure thing."

"Where's Terry?" Bill asked. "She was supposed to be here to run over the new material for the Saturday night show."

"She'll be along. Don't worry about that girl. She's a peach."

"Sure. A peach that doesn't mind who takes a bite out of her!" Bill observed, nastily.

"What's gotten into you?"

"Come on! You know Laura took off today."

"So...she'll be back."

"Anyway, I have a hangover."

Don looked strangely at him for a long moment, then said: "Since when did you over drink?"

"Since today!" Bill snapped back, standing and moving to the bandstand.

"Let's run through a few numbers!" he told the men.

For twenty minutes they whipped through a pile of new arrangements.

They were taking a break when Terry Anson breezed in, and behind her came Hanson, serious faced, a cigar clamped in his tight mouth. He walked up to the stand with Terry but didn't follow her onto it.

Bill turned and nodded to Terry and then looked at Hanson. "What brings you?"

"Just wanted to check that everything was okay."

"Why shouldn't it be?" Bill cried, a little surprised by his agent's attitude.

"Well, this guy is coming to see what you fellows can blow and I just want to give out the old pep talk!"

"Save it, Hanson!" Bill told him in a cool voice. He didn't like the man, and never had.

Hanson was a good agent, though, and that was all that really counted. He wanted to get ahead and that was the end of the matter. Hanson could pull the right strings and make the right connections jump.

"Just blow good, Billy-boy!" Hanson growled, turning and leaving.

"I do that all the time. So just stop the lecture!" Bill snapped, annoyed.

"That wasn't nice of you!" Terry told him, "Hanson drove me all the way over here!"

Don gave Bill a knowing look and he got the message. Terry had spent the night with Hanson. That was Terry for you. Climb her way up the ladder through the bedchambers of anybody willing to pull her pants off.

"Okay, let's run through your numbers, Terry," Bill ordered, turning toward the girl.

She looked at him in a strange way and then extended a few lead sheet arrangements, smiling. "Roughed in. I figure you guys can ad-lib it behind me."

She made it a point to touch his fingers as she passed the papers into his hands.

"Get Laura off?" she asked.

"What do you think?"

"I just asked. Guess you'll be lonely."

"That's my affair!" Bill snapped.

"I'm not making a pass, if that's what you mean."

"Pretty hard to tell when you're serious and... well!" He shrugged.

"When I make a pass, you'll know it, honey."

"Just keep 'em to yourself, I don't need that kind of thing right now," Bill snapped back a bit nastily.

She gave him a double-take, but strangely didn't say anything about that.

It was Don who objected with: "Look, you don't have to knock everybody. We know you're pushed out of shape, but...cool it, man!"

30

Bill relaxed. "Sorry. Hangover and things have me."

They started working through Terry's numbers. She stopped a couple of times to indicate that she wanted something either slower or faster. Each time she leaned as close as she could to Bill, and made it a point to touch his arm with her fingers. He ignored the implication.

It was about seven when they broke for dinner.

"Be back at nine, sharp and we'll go on early so we can have a little warm up!" Bill told them. Then he turned to Don: "Want company for dinner?"

The bass man nodded.

Terry quickly stepped up. "How about a third party?'

Don started to nod agreement, but Bill cut him off with a wave of his hand. "Not tonight!"

Terry looked disappointed, but she didn't object. Only shrugged her shoulders and bounced away.

Dinner was good, but Bill didn't notice. The only thing that he could see was Laura's form.

At one point Bill said: "Damn woman. Terry keeps touching and making subtle plays…"

"She's harmless about that, and you know it. That's her manner, her way of being friendly."

"I'm not in the mood."

"What's with you, Bill?' Don asked.

"I don't know. Have that terrible feeling in the pit of my guts that keeps saying that I'll never see Laura again. Really scary."

"You off your nut?"

"Sure. It's silly. But some things a person just can't make logic out of. Ever since Laura got this harebrained idea of going home for Christmas...well, I've been on edge. Now...I don't know. Let's drop it!"

The subject turned to their work. The prospect of a recording contract had Don all excited. "This will mean the difference of just getting by, and really swinging. Hanson has the contacts!"

"Syndicate connected!" Bill pointed out.

"So what? In this business there's a lot of under the table politics. You can't get away from it; and Hanson is one guy that knows all the tricks." Don looked evenly at Bill, a serious expression on his face. "You haven't liked the man ever since I introduced you to him."

"Just a feeling. I've always had the idea that if anybody crossed him he wouldn't like it at all!"

"Who likes to be crossed?"

"That's not what I mean, Don. I have the feeling he'd blow his lid! Dangerously so!"

"Oh, come on. You're down on everything tonight. What you need is a woman to cheer you up. Why don't you take Terry up on her offer?"

"Nothing doing!"

"You know she's got hot tingles for you. She'd blow a chorus with you any day or night. What would Laura know about it? A meaningless number or so with the lady. She's great! A lovely kid. Everybody likes her. She'll blow your horn even jazzier than you do!" The man laughed at that. "And, quite frankly, I like lookin' down her boobies. She's got—"

"Oh, shut up! And if I were to do that...well...you know damned well Terry would blab all over the place!"

"I think you have the wrong idea about her, Bill.

She might be a bit of a free spirit and all that right now, but one of these days some guy will grab her and I have the feeling she'll make one hell of a good wife. Loyal as hell, devoted. She's like any other woman, complicated, sure, but a great friend and somebody you can rely on. Even if she's a blatantly wild flirt. That's just part of her personality."

"Then marry her!" Bill told him angrily.

"She doesn't even know I exist! And anyway you know me and broads that work in the business. Hands off, that's me. I'll take 'em from the audience groupies. But you're different. You got your hands on every girl you met."

"Before Laura!" Bill remarked, dryly. *"Let's* drop the subject of women. Be a pal?"

"Sure, sure."

They finished dinner in almost complete silence. After paying the bill, they walked out onto the street, starting back for the club. On the corner was a newsboy, holding out a paper with heavy headlines, and shouting:

"Plane crash near New York! Read all about it! Thirty people killed! Read all about it!" Bill didn't pay any attention at first, until they started passing the boy and he happened to glance at the paper and saw the headlines. They read:

"PLANE CRASH, NO SURVIVORS!"

It sank in. The subtitle: "New York Flight 705 crashes outside of airport."

A choking yell burst from his lips and he felt his face drain. A gnarled hand twisted in his stomach, knotting it into a painful ache. He felt sweat break out on his forehead.

Flight 705. That was Laura's flight!

Bill looked at the headline for a long time, his face distorted with pain and agony. It wasn't until Don nudged him that he realized what he had been doing.

"What's wrong?" Don asked, concern coloring his voice.

"Laura…on that plane," Bill answered in a dull, lifeless tone. It took several seconds before he could realize fully what it meant. That he would never see Laura again; that he would never get married to her; that he would never hold her in his arms.

Suddenly a yell broke from his lips. It was filled with the insanity of complete and utter hopelessness. Before Don could stop him, Bill was running down the street.

He didn't realize what he was doing, or where he was going for a long time. All he knew, when awareness began to return, was that he'd been running for a long distance, how much time he had been blacked out, he didn't know. It was dark, now. The evening had settled down on the city.

He was walking now, but his body ached and his mind was still screaming inwardly that Laura was dead.

He didn't break pace, but turned and walked into a bar that was at the end of the street. He sat down on a stool and ordered a whiskey, but before the bartender had taken two steps away from him, he added: "Make that a triple shot."

The man looked sharply at him, but started fixing the drink and in a few seconds he was gulping it. When it was finished he ordered another.

34

Twenty minutes later he was pretty high and working on his fourth single. After the first triple he'd calmed down a little, because the whiskey was finally beginning to create a numbing band around his head He just sat there at the bar, trying to think of nothing but the whiskey. Not trying to think of Laura or that she was dead and would never be in his arms again. He didn't think about the job that he had to do that night. Work was a finished item for him; that much he knew.

He looked down into the small shot glass and wondered how many he would have to drink before the world closed completely around his consciousness. That's what he wanted. It was the only thing he would ever want again. Without Laura, nothing mattered.

Nothing!

He had known her for only a few months, but that had been the beginning of life for Bill. Up to that time he'd been bumming from one town to another working either with a group of his own, or for somebody else, making an existence and nothing more. It had been drinking, playing, women and eating. And plenty of women.

Until Laura. There had been something very different about her; something that had captured him from the first moment he had seen her sitting at the small table looking at him as he played a long solo. She had smiled shyly up at him but had dropped her eyes when they'd met his.

Later, during a break, he'd gone and introduced himself, working the general line that got him into most women's pants. But even though she was more than eager to let him sit there and talk and buy her drinks, she wasn't about to let him take her home. Let alone cut into her pants. That was the first thing different about Laura. Sure, many women weren't so eager to let him make the point with them. But those kind were different from Laura. They weren't about to let him buy them drinks; sit and talk, but nothing else. Any other woman who would let him buy drinks and then not pay off later with a little playing around in the bedchambers would have burned Bill to the core. And that was the second thing about Laura. He couldn't forget her. And she was there at the club the next night, listening and watching. He sat with her and talked, bought her drinks and then she went home, alone, in a taxi cab, like the night before. It wasn't until a week had gone by before she would let him drive her home.

She lived in a small room, in a small apartment house that was modern and expensive, with a pool in the back. She just said goodbye at the door, nothing more. They had held hands walking up to her room, but that was as intimate as Laura was about to let him get, then. Two nights later she had let him kiss her goodnight. The next evening she had returned the kiss with all the fire and passion that a woman could possibly generate.

Later, all that night, he had been fired by that one kiss. It had been electric and overpowering.

She hadn't been to the club the next night. When she didn't turn up three nights in a row, he had gone to her place and rung the bell. She was in. But a little afraid of him. Not until later did he learn that she had stopped coming to see him because of the overwhelming response that had moved her that last evening they'd seen each other.

Somehow the conversation had turned directly to sex, then, and she had quite openly come out and stated that she'd never had a man before and that he was the first and only man that she'd ever considered having an affair with.

That had surprised him slightly, but he'd managed to hide his reaction.

It wasn't until a week later, after having seen her every night after work and in the evening before work, that he made any passes at her. And the night he did, accidentally in the car, when his hand made the mistake of brushing her breasts, she had responded fully. After that the affair had started, and a month later he had asked her to marry him. She was the kind of woman that he'd always been looking for; the kind that didn't put out to every *Joe* that wanted her, but who wasn't really afraid when the right man came along.

Quiet and sure of herself in some ways, and in the other ways a little fearful and childlike. And now she was dead and he could never hold her in his arms again, he could never make love to her, he could never marry her.

He gulped the whiskey, draining the glass, and ordered another.

"Don't you think you've had enough, buddy!" the bartender said.

"Look! I'm paying. I want some more. If you don't give it to me, I'll go someplace else."

"Okay, okay, buddy anything you say!" the man told him.

A moment later he had the glass back, filled. He looked gloomily at it for a long while. Then, just as he was about to drain it in one gulp, a woman's voice sounded at his side.

"Say, you look like you need a friend," she observed, sitting down next to him.

Chapter Four

It was the silky sound of her voice that made him turn and look. What he saw surprised him. The woman was tall, blonde, and almost beautiful. Not quite beautiful, but extremely attractive. Her lips were full and bright red. Her cheeks high, with a narrowness to her face that was interesting. What he could see of the bulge of her breasts under the tight fitting woman's suit, revealed a voluptuous figure that any man would look at twice. He wondered what she was doing at a crummy place like this, trying to pick up a man.

He didn't say anything to her. His expression was completely blank all the time he stared her figure up and down.

"Well, don't you want company?' she asked in a biting, almost irritated tone of voice.

She started to stand.

"Wait!" he blurted out, before he realized what he was doing. He didn't want to offend her, yet on the other hand he hadn't decided that he was interested in being with a woman. Oh, she wasn't coming right out and saying: take me off on your charger and ravish my body; though it was her meaning. She was subtler than that. But that was where it would end.

She paused and gave him a startled look.

He thought fast for a moment and then decided. He was drunk enough to not care. And, maybe a woman's body would blur pain. Drink it up and then bang it up that might not be such a bad idea. There wasn't any reason that he should be alone in his misery, and the idea of sex teased his half drunk mind. He smiled automatically and said: "I'm sorry. You just surprised me a little. Sure. Sit down. Let me buy you a drink."

"Well, what do you think of that?" she laughed. "Quite a quick change. For a moment there I thought that you weren't interested in little ol' me."

He didn't answer that, only nodded.

"Well, since you're buying, I'll have a martini, if it's all the same with you?"

"Why not? They all cost the same," he commented dryly.

"Oh, I know that. Just that a lot of the guys around this joint don't understand. What I mean is, they think I'm trying to be classy." She smiled at him. "Or something like that."

"Well, you are classy!"

"Not so classy, honey, that you can't expect a lot of fun. I'm a fun girl, out looking for a lot of the same."

She touched his arm. "My, you're a strong fella, you are!"

"All the better to overwhelm you?" he chuckled, playfully as she withdrew her hand. "I suspect."

"I'm not about to challenge you on that point. And you certainly don't have to be a powerhouse with me. Just a nice guy looking for a nice time with a lady."

"Well, nice to know you, then," he commented, forcing himself to get into the mood of the thing.

Why not? His mind was drifting, slipping into a long patterned thinking process. He knew exactly how to play this game, without even considering which riff he needed to adlib. It was like blowing a chorus of music, just improvising to the offered-up cords.

"And you do seem to be a neat, classy lady, at that!"

"Say, that's nice of you to say so," she laughed. Then seriously she asked: "You really think so?"

"Look, lady, I wouldn't say so if I didn't mean it. And just look at your dress!"

She laughed again, and this time he realized that she'd been stringing him along.

"Like the dress?"

"Sure. What's not to like about it. And, baby, what's in it ain't all that bad, either."

"Is that the best you can do?" she smiled.

"Well, I haven't heard the tune, so can't make any judgments about the arrangement."

"Arrangement?"

"Oh, well, whatever's under the covers."

She laughed at that. "Boy, you come right out and blow a lady away."

"Not yet. Not yet."

"Oh, is that what you have in mind?"

"Who knows. But I don't review a play I haven't seen in the flesh!"

She laughed again. 'You're outrageous!"

"Shocking?"

"Hardly, just smoothly ribald!"

41

"Is that a dirty word?"

"Ripe balled? Gee, I don't know, honey. Are you?" She looked pointedly down. "My, I just can't review what I don't see."

"Now who's being down right *risqué*, lady?"

"Oh, is that one of those naughty French words?"

"I suppose. Risqué could be considered French for dirt-tay!"

They both laughed at that as her martini came. She lifted the drink and said: "Bottoms up?"

"Really?"

"I would hope so, funny man!"

For a moment he almost had a feeling of liking her. She seemed to show a little inner intelligence.

The bartender stepped up, his eyebrows raised slightly.

"Martini for the lady, and another straight shot for myself."

The man left.

"You've been really belting them down," she told him in a light voice.

"Sure, why not?" Then he snapped, "Something wrong with that?"

"Just noticed. That's the reason I—what I mean is, you look like you don't belong here…and the way you're taking the straight booze you must have problems."

"I have problems."

"Don't we all?"

He gave her a quick, almost annoyed look, but she was cheery-eyed.

"Honey, I'm a fun lady…so don't take me too seriously."

42

The bartender returned with the drinks, and Bill paid the man. Taking the whiskey, he gulped it down quickly, not even tasting the reaction. He was beyond the point of feeling the heat go down his throat and even though he didn't show any real outward signs of being drunk, his head was beginning to slowly swim. And that's the way he wanted it.

The conversational exchange had been on automatic, much like it would have been if his horn was pressed up against his lips and he was blowing a sad song through it. All running on some inner surge of power that made everything focused and right on pitch.

He turned and looked at the woman, very carefully. She was attractive enough, that much he had noticed before. But there was a look about her that spelled class. She didn't belong in the bar any more than he did. This was a dive and she wasn't the barmaid type. She was the kind of woman that people read about in the high society section of the Sunday papers. There was a sparkling necklace around her creamy white throat. He didn't really know anything about jewels, but it looked like the real thing. *If it was...?* He didn't even try to finish that thought.

She was here to be picked up and that was all that should matter to him or anybody else interested in banging her in the rack.

What was he doing sitting there, thinking about giving it to a broad, when the woman he loved was lying dead....

He didn't allow himself to finish that thought. It was too dangerous for his emotional sanity. The only thing that counted, now, was pure and utter escape. He'd worry about everything else the next day or the next week. Maybe next year. Or never. Right then he didn't really care. Didn't give a damn!

"Say, what're you thinking?" she asked, giving him an odd look.

"Just...thinking."

"Why the strange look?"

He let his eyes sweep over her body. "What you have under there?"

She smiled. "You want to find out, is that it?"

He suddenly shrugged, eyes focusing, then his mind attempted to make sense out of what was happening. Suddenly he covered his face with shaking hands.

For a very long time there was silence. Then she said: "What's wrong with you?"

He lowered his hand, gazed blankly at her, not even seeing the woman's face at all.

"What's wrong with you?" she repeated, almost angry, when he didn't answer.

He shook his head from side to side, trying to clear it, trying to focus on the woman. Finally she formed into a shape and he just stared at her for a long time.

"Is there something wrong with you?" she asked, again sounded quite annoyed. "Are you drunk?"

"What's it to you!" he asked, tiredly. He wanted her to go away. "Why don't you just find some sober stud to spread out your goodies!"

"Well!" she snapped angrily, looking at him for a short moment before standing and walking away.

That was the end of that, he thought, bitterly, ordering another drink. *It was drunk time!*

44

Drink, drink, my happy laddies,
Drink and know of sin!
Drink to the sexy Ladies,
That you're 'bout to win!

He hadn't thought about that one since his college days, and didn't know why it had come to his mind.

There was another part of it, he thought drunkenly, something about....

He laughed lightly at first, and then suddenly the laugh burst violently out of his lips. It was several minutes before he could gain control of himself and when he did he saw that several people were looking in his direction. Some with interest on their faces, others with a touch of contempt. One face smiled at him. It was feminine looking, almost like a woman's, and from the way it smiled he could see that it thought like a woman and desired like a woman.

"Okay, buddy, what's the bit?" the bartender asked, leaning over the bar and peering into his eyes.

"Another drink!" he managed to blurt out almost evenly.

"I think you've had enough!"

"I want another drink!"

"Not here, mister!" the man said firmly.

"Say, what kind of joint is this?" he demanded, starting to stand and lean over the bar toward the other man.

"Look, mister, No more drinks for you. Go some other place!"

Angrily Bill jerked from the bar and then rushed for the door. His walk was unsteady, but he was still able to move. He wanted to get to the point where he wasn't conscious of anything.

To another bar! he shouted inwardly.

There was one down the block and he staggered toward it. Suddenly he came to a stop and forced control over himself. He could either act drunk, or take it very carefully and put on the sober act.

His steps took on the look of a loping gait, easy swinging, but carefully made. He mentally hummed a musical riff, his feet tapping rhythmically under him to that beat. This worked just fine. His movement was steady, controlled. Finally he was sitting on another barstool, in the second saloon.

Drunk, drunk us happy laddies,
Drunk, knee-deep in play,
Drunk with a sexy Lady,
That we're 'bout to lay!

* * * * * * *

Don Jenson looked nervously around at the other musicians and then sighed: "Bill ran out!"

"What the hell!" the piano man cried.

"What happened?' the drummer asked.

"Saw a headline and went crazy. I started after him, but he was running too fast. I figured he would turn up by now. Anyway I went back to the newsman and read the headlines. A plane crashed just outside of New York this evening. On the casualty list was Laura Jones' name!"

The others stared at him in shock. Jack the

drummer opened his mouth and then closed it. The piano-man shuffled his feet. It was the combo's sax man, Walt, who said, "God! Now what?"

"A million dollar question!" Don pointed out. "We have to go on with the show. There's nothing else to do."

"Without Billy?' the sax man asked, startled.

"You have a better idea?" Don countered. "I'll call Terry and have her come in for tonight; that might take the customers' minds off the fact that the feature player isn't here!"

"What'll Hanson say?" the sax man asked.

"Good, God!" Don choked. "I'd forgotten about that. The recording bit!"

He sighed and then said: "We can't do anything but hope Bill snaps out of the shock. Maybe he'll show up!"

* * * * * * *

Terry sat up in bed as the phone rang, a little dazed. She'd been in the middle of a heavy sleep and she couldn't clear her mind at first. Finally she realized where the ringing came from and reached for the receiver on the night stand.

"Hello?" she said sleepily.

"It's Don. We have a problem...Billy disappeared!" came Don's startling opening statement.

"What!" she jerked up in bed, completely awake.

"There was a plane crash—"

Her throat choked and she blurted out, interrupting the man: "He's not hurt!"

"No! No! Laura. She was on the plane that

crashed outside of New York!"

Then he told her what little he knew about it. She just sat there, slowly gaining a strange feeling of happiness; and as it grew there was an undercurrent of guilt that she should be happy that somebody had died. After she hung up, saying that she would come down to the club right away, she sat for a long time just thinking.

It was horrible that Laura had died. That much she could really feel. The idea of anybody dying. Plus Laura had been a very special, nice lady, even if she had totally captured Bill into her love-web. It was difficult to know what to feel. Part of Terry was terribly shaken by the other woman's death, and at the same time there was the other side that understood what a chance it opened up for her.

It gave her another chance at Bill Carter and he would be in a more willing mood to listen to her open offer. Now he could be hers for the taking. And how she wanted him.

For several minutes she sat there shivering, tearing streaming down her face. It was horrible to think of Laura dying that way. But there wasn't anything anybody could do about that, except accept the truth.

Literally shaking herself, she wiped the tears away, and decided to simply deal with the realities. Life was giving her a second chance to win Bill— and she wasn't about to blow that away!

She'd been slightly in love with Bill ever since she'd joined the group, and now she saw her first real chance to get what she was after. Bill Carter in marriage or any other way she could have him. She had tried hard to keep from showing her feelings for the man because of Laura; but now things had changed dramatically. It wasn't a matter of not caring about Laura's death, but more an acceptance that now she had a chance to win him for herself.

Cruel as it might seem, Terry realized, life had to go on, and now there was a chance for her to move in to the void Laura's death created.

"You're being terrible," she told herself, reluctantly trying to wipe away such thoughts. But they kept flooding in. A rushing joy filled her; she had a chance, finally—and she would make the most of it.

From this moment on she was going to play it hardball for Bill Carter's affections! No matter what she had to do.

She slid out of bed, walked to the bathroom, undressed, and took a shower.

Then it was on to the club!

Chapter Five

Bill was wondering where he was, it looked so much like a thousand other dumps. Another bar, another room of people.

He stepped to the bar, looked at the bartender, and then told him, bluntly: "Nothing but the best!"

"Best what?' the man asked suspiciously.

"Whiskey. What do you think? That's what I've been drinking." He broke off and then tried to laugh. For a moment he'd forgotten where he was, thinking he was at the first bar. "Whiskey. A double shot, please."

Oh, Laura, Laura, where are you! God! How could I live without you?

Think about something different! he commanded his mind.

What?

Anything!

What was the third verse of that drinking song? he asked himself.

He tried to remember and then finally realized that there wasn't any third verse. The drink came and he downed half of it and sat there, staring blindly at the top of the bar counter.

He had to think of something besides poor, dear,

and sweet, wonderful, Laura Jones.

> *Drinking all day all night,*
> *Drinking from morn to noon,*
> *We're sure to have a hell'va fight,*
> *And it's certain to happen soon.*
> *Because there is a lady fair,*
> *And there are two of us,*
> *We're not about of her to share,*
> *And that's one hell'va fuss!*
>
> *So Drinking to her, we are to do,*
> *Drinking for love's own sake.*
> *Drinking 'till she, one of us woo,*
> *To touch, to kiss, to take.*
> *And if the maid, she is not willing,*
> *Though she be more than right,*
> *With booze she will be filling,*
> *Till she's good and tight!*
> *And one of us, for sure will take,*
> *Her ripe full breasts in hand;*
> *Because we're drunk and on the make,*
> *Her target we're sure to land.*

His drink was finished and he ordered a second, feeling his whole body beginning to swim in a sea of dizziness, until it was hard to be fully aware of his surroundings. He knew that there was another full whiskey shot glass in his hands, but he didn't know if it was the second or third. There was a hazy blur spinning before his eyes.

"Wanna buy a gal a drink?' some voice asked him.

He turned and looked, hardly seeing the face sit-

51

ting on the barstool next to where he sat.

"Sure thing, Lady!" he exclaimed in a loud and drunken voice. "A drunk for the Shady!" Then he added under his breath, not really knowing he'd said it:

"With booze she will be filling,
Till she's good and tight!"

* * * * * * *

Hanson glared at them, his eyes narrowing:
"What kind of fool trick is that?"
"I'm telling you the truth. Bill saw the headlines and then blew!" Don told him.
"He can't do that to me!" Hanson roared, wildly waving his hands in the air.
"Look, Bill was crazy about her!"
Hanson relaxed, his face softening slightly. "Okay, I guess there's nothing we can do about it, now." He sighed and then added: "When the boy comes in, tell me. If he doesn't...well, I'll have to make up some story about it. Stall!"
"Why don't you tell the man the truth?" Terry suggested, her hands coming to her waist.
Hanson slowly let his eyes run the full length of her figure that was tightly squeezed by the silken blue dress she was wearing. They stopped at the bulge of her neckline.
"You kidding?" he asked, nastily.
"Why not? What better reason for a guy to disappear than when he hears about his girl's death!"
Finally it seemed to sink into the man's hard emotions that what the girl suggested was true. He

shrugged. "So, it's a good idea! I'll tell him the truth!" He turned toward Don, his face hard and serious: "But you, buster, get him back by tomorrow night!"

* * * * * * *

Bill was aware of a cheap apartment. The walls looked dim and faraway, but he had the impression that they were grease-smeared and old. There was a dingy feeling about the place. He didn't know where he was, but that didn't really matter. And he didn't have any clear idea how or when he had gotten there.

It was the woman's nude body, and its wild, hungry, demanding force that had brought partial awareness. Her tongue was surging in and out of his mouth and he could feel the sweaty pressure of her skin against his.

He was breathing hard, and his body ached with desire. A throbbing excitement was rushing through him, racing the blood and burning his brain He felt his hands being led down to hard small breasts that seemed to move eagerly up again his fingers. He responded, automatically, heard moans utter from a woman's mouth.

He tried to look at the face, but couldn't quite focus on it. From what little he could make out, it was plain and unattractive. But that didn't make any difference, because her body was much too active to make him really care about anything. He knew she had taken him in her, he could feel the warm gripping of her flesh tugging and pulling savagely.

It was all a kind of nightmare, an erotic hell

53

grasping him like some furious vice.

He didn't know what he was doing in this woman's apartment—or was it some flea-bitten hotel room? He didn't care.

Suddenly she jerked hard and firmly up against him. After that he didn't think about much except the automatic reaction of his body. The world clouded a little and then he was aware of lying on his back, looking up at the ceiling.

If unconsciousness had captured him, then released its hold on his mind, he didn't know. Everything was a blur.

He closed his eyes for only a moment and then felt an eager clawing hand groping along his stomach and then moving to his thigh. And all at once a body slid over on top of his and he felt the demanding hunger of a female animal anxiously taking the food of her desire.

He passed out a little after that. When he awoke he looked around the room. His head was splitting and his throat dry.

The place was old and cheap. The wallpaper was spotted and at several places was peeling from the wall. There was only the bed and a dresser in the small room. In the distance he was aware of sounds. It took some time to place them and make out what they meant. They came from the room beyond the wall behind him. The thrashing sounds of bedsprings left nothing to the imagination, and if it had, the moans and groans of the two people destroyed all doubt of what was going on.

He felt a sickness in his gut. Then he noticed a bottle on the floor next to the bed. Reaching down, he picked it up and started drinking from it; thirstily, desperately. Then he heard a slight movement on the bed next to him and turned to look.

The woman was in her late forties, thin and quite unattractive. Her eyes deep set and her forehead wide. The breasts on her chest were hardly more than oversize nipples that spread from the hard and worn points. Suddenly her eyes opened and she smiled up at him.

"Say, you awake again!" she cried, reaching out. "Balls alive, you fuck a girl wild!"

Revulsion clawed in his stomach, sending stabs of pain and disgust through his whole body. *How could he have ever picked up a woman like this?*

He gulped on the bottle again and a blur settled through his system. He felt a little better, but not good enough. He gulped again and then was aware of a caressing hand moving along his thigh.

He looked, startled.

The woman was bright-eyed and already breathing heavily. She looked at him for a moment and then suddenly squirmed closer. Her arms circled his body, drawing her form tightly against his. Her lips brushed aside the bottle in his hands and then contacted his mouth. The anxious demanding action of her tongue forced his lips open and then he felt it surge deep into his mouth, jerking and tasting and seeking deeper union. She shuddered convulsively against him and suddenly he found himself drunkenly responding to her coarse lovemaking.

Hands reached down between them and before he realized what was happening the woman had joined their bodies with one forceful thrust.

It was fast and demanding. Quick and over before he had even realized that it had begun.

He reached for the bottle in disgust and she reached once more for him.

He drank deep and then turned his attention to her active body. She was devouring him with her mouth. Part of him tried to move away, but it was a weak action that seemed to encourage her to more frantic attempting to keep hold of him. And she was either stronger or more sober or more demanding, for he found himself sinking into some deep well, all at once helpless.

How long he stayed with the woman he didn't really know. It was through a blur of red that he moved, letting her make love to him and then he finally smothering himself against her in a desperate attempt to escape all reality.

The nightmare continued, more unreal than real.

It was as if time stood momentarily still as he escaped in her hard, coarse, demanding kisses and caresses. Drinking. There was a lot of drinking. He fell asleep and when he woke, there was another bottle at the side of the bed. He dove into the liquor, draining it slowly, and keeping in a continued state of drunkenness. And the woman wouldn't stop long in her greedy need. Maybe she was a nympho, or simply sex-starved. It didn't matter. He didn't even care any longer. He drank and let her use him every way her mind could think of; hands, lips and body interchangeable machines that kept assaulting him time and again.

Finally the disgust and sickness overcame his body until there wasn't anything left but a retching of his gut. That continued until it had emptied itself. It was as if watching from the outside of his body, not able to control it, not able to think for it. He

56

retched, with the numbing sickness convulsing through his every cell and nerve. His head was cut into a series of throbbing and pulsing aches, and finally the tight bands closed in around his skull until only blackness was left.

He dreamed through the sleep.

He was lying on a beach with Laura. Her body was warm under his, throbbing with life and passion. Her breasts, large and full, but delicate, matching the beauty of her tiny form, pumped against his chest. Her arms, lean and slender, caressed his back, pulling his body tighter to her.

He felt her move against him, hungrily. Her lips, wide and moist clamped to his as their bodies moved rhythmically together. It was an endless riff of continual vamping time and again, a lovely melody that surrounded his very soul. He felt her shudder against him once more and then go limp.

For a while he lay there, thinking that she was only sexually exhausted. Then finally he looked down at her body and saw that it was twisted in death.

A choke sobbed in his throat and he slowly moved away and picked up her distorted form in his arms and started walking down the sand toward the water. He walked into the water, the waves lapping first at his feet and then above his knees. A large wave shot over his head, spinning his body, but he managed to keep hold of Laura. Then he was walking again. Now the water was as high as his chest and a few moments later up to his neck.

He kept walking until he felt himself completely covered with the soothing water of death.

His lungs began to burst. They became heavy in

him and then started to pulse with agony until he thought he couldn't stand it any longer.

He was screaming. His throat hurt from screaming.

Suddenly his eyes opened and he saw his surroundings. He was lying on the dirty bed in the dirty room. The covers were half on the bed and half on the floor. There was a sick smell to the air and he vaguely knew what it was.

Looking around he saw that the room was empty, outside of himself. His clothes were on the floor in the corner. Several whiskey bottles were cluttering the floor around them.

Slowly he stood and then fell forward across the bed.

How long he lay there he didn't know. He passed out for a time and then slowly awakened. His head was hammering with pain. His whole body was in a vise of steel that pinched every nerve into a burning flame of agony.

It took a long time for him to get the strength to get up. Longer still to step slowly over to his pile of clothes, walking carefully in order not to jar his head.

Then he dressed.

He had to get out of there.

He had to get a drink.

Chapter Six

Billy Carter walked the streets of the town for several hours before he stepped into an all night diner. After a meal of a thick steak and coffee, he started to pay the check and discovered that his wallet was missing. Panic shot through him for a moment. His mind felt sick. The first thought was that he would have to wash dishes for the rest of the night, or be locked up in jail.

Then a second thought occurred to him, and even though he mentally repelled by it, there wasn't anything else to do. He tried to smile at the waitress and then said in an even voice: "Gosh, I'm sorry. I left my wallet at home. I'll have to call my buddy."

The woman gave him a double take and nodded knowingly.

"Okay, mister, what kind of deal is this?" She eyed his thin beard that was at least a couple days old and then said: "You been on the bum?"

Her tone was insulting.

"Oh, come on. I'll pay you. Do you have a phone so that I can call this friend of mine?"

She stared coldly at him for a moment and then nodded, pointing her finger toward the back. "Over there, but don't try walking out on us!"

He started to reply to that remark and then decided that it wasn't worth his effort. It would be hard enough to call Don Jenson; that would take all the emotional energy he could get. The last thing that he wanted to do was see or talk to any of the men in the band.

That was the first time he'd thought about his job and the way he'd walked out on it. Vaguely he wondered exactly what his buddies had thought and how the gig had worked out without him. He decided that his men knew how to handle a job, with or without a leader. Don no doubt had taken over.

He paused on his way to the phone and then turned. On second thought, he decided not to pay. Let them throw him in jail.

Then he reconsidered that idea. If they got him in jail it would be a stretch without booze and he'd have to face himself, and he wasn't ready for that. Better to call Don and let it go at that.

He remembered he didn't have any change and went to the waitress and asked for some. She reluctantly gave it to him. A moment later he had dialed. It was several seconds before he heard somebody pick up the other end of the line.

"Gable Hotel," a voice said.

"Can I speak to Don Jenson in Room 702?"

"Just a minute, I'll see if he's in."

It was several seconds before he heard Don's sleepy voice. "Hello? Who the hell is—?"

"Don, this is Bill."

"Bill! Good God, man, where've you been? We've been looking for you for days!"

"How many?" he asked, just slightly interested.

"Three. You just disappeared. We got as far as

where you must have picked up some broad!" Then Don's voice changed. "You all right? Where are you?"

"At Davy's Diner on Main and Second."

"Stay right there. I'll come and get you."

"I can't leave. Don't have any money."

"Don't move. See you!" The phone went dead. It was twenty minutes before Don Jenson arrived. He paid the bill without hardly saying a word to Bill, then the two of them went out to the bass man's car. Once they were driving along the street, Don turned toward Bill and said: "You want to talk about it?"

"No," was Bill's only dry comment.

"Look, Bill..."

"No lectures, Don!" he snapped, tensing his hands into solid fists. His mouth was dry and his guts aching. He needed a drink.

"When you ran out the other evening I started to run after you and then stopped, went back and got one of the papers. I...." Don stopped and then after taking a deep breath continued: "I know what this must have meant to you. But...but you can't stop living!"

"Can't I?" Bill demanded, bitterly. "Give me one good reason."

"You're alive."

"Yeah." He didn't finish the statement, but his tone of voice carried the finish: *I wish I wasn't!*

"Laura wouldn't want you—"

"Don't talk about her!" The hardness in his voice caused the other man to remain quiet.

Silence carried them for several miles and then Don broke it again. "The boys have been worried.

So has Terry—she worried something terrible!"

There was a vague, strange feeling that welled up over him upon mention of Terry. That last time he'd seen her was the last night Laura had been alive. And she'd said the woman probably had a thing for him. Terry Anson was one tiny, compact a ball of sexual energy. She sang a song from her guts in such a way that most of the customers in the club, each night, kept flashing smiles in her direction. She'd gone out with a few men from the audience. The men in the combo were all married except Don and himself. Don wasn't interested in Terry's type. He kept to broads outside of the business. "Too touchy when you cut into a girl working with you!" he had said as way of explanation. But Bill had never been one to care much where the social life came from, B.L: *Before Laura.*

Now it was A.L.: *After Laura.* Where was he going to head? He tried to think that one out, but he didn't get very far because Don's voice cut into his thoughts:

"...and what about the job? I can't stall any longer. They want the feature player: *you!* And if they can't have you...they'll drop the contract, and we're out on our ear."

"You think that makes any difference to me?" Bill asked, nastily.

"Look, Bill. You don't just have yourself to consider. There're others. Jack and Walt, they have kids. Manny well, he can keep going for a while. Get a gig of his own someplace. As for myself I need the money, but..."

"But you're a buddy!" The tone of his voice was bitter, but he meant it. Don had been a buddy for years; they'd seen a lot of bad times together.

"What are you going to do?"

"You can handle the group."

"I can't. We're out if you don't turn up...and soon!" Don said firmly. "And that's the truth."

"I just can't."

"You have to."

"What if I'd had some money? What if that bitch I'd been racking it with hadn't split with my wallet and money? I wouldn't be...here! I don't want to talk about it!" Bill snapped, angrily, looking through the windshield for a bar. "I need a drink!"

"You've had enough!"

"Hell, Don!"

"Look, when you go on a bender like this you've had enough!"

"Either I get a drink now, or I split at the first stop light!"

Don sighed and then said, reluctantly. "Okay, man we dig into a hole...maybe I can talk some sense to you over a little booze."

"Sure, you try that, pal!"

Don brought the car into the first parking spot he could find and the two of them got out and walked down half a block to the corner where there was a small saloon.

A few minutes later Bill had downed his first shot and ordered another, a double this time.

"Don't you think you're hitting it a little heavy?" Don objected when the second drink came and he started downing it.

"Shut up!" was Bill's only reply, finishing the drink and looking across at his friend.

"Come on, Bill, this is Don, your all time buddy.

You don't have to turn me on and off. I just want to help. I know how it is. There was a girl once in my life, too if you remember. But I snapped out of it."

"After a bender of two years!"

Don was silent after that remark; his face had become slightly white, his lips compressed. Then suddenly he cheered up, smiling: "So it took me a while to come out. Anyway, she hadn't been worth it. I realized that, finally. She walked out on me, and I was lucky."

"Yeah. That's the difference. Laura and me were getting married. Things were perfect. Now they're blasted to hell!"

"Look, Bill. Don't think you're the only guy with hurts. Remember the woman I loved—and damn it all, so help me, still love—is still breathing, pulsing with life, and in the arms of some other slob!" Don cried, bitterly, leaning forward, his face serious and set. "It might sound hard, but at least you won't have to face that!"

"Oh, God!" Bill sobbed, suddenly, his hands pressing into his face. He sat there for a long time trying to control the overwhelming emotion that choked a hardness in his throat. He felt his chest heaving and heard the sound of half sobs breaking from his lips. Normally he didn't get affected by anything like that—sober he would have been able to control himself. But not drunk. Finally, though, he managed. His hands slid away from his face and he tried to focus his blurry vision on Don's features.

"You through feeling sorry for yourself?" his friend asked coldly.

"What's wrong with you?" Bill demanded in a tortured voice.

"Nothing! It's you. I know how it is. But you can go through life feeling sorry for yourself, or face up to it like a man. Sure, you don't like what happened. It was a dirty trick of fate. But what can you do about it? Can you bring Laura back? Can you change what happened?"

"That's not the point!"

"What is the point? Destroy yourself? End it all? It would be easier to put a gun to your head and pull the trigger. And a lot more painless. But you don't have the courage to do even that!"

"Leave me alone!" he managed to choke out.

"No! I won't leave you alone. I won't let you slowly destroy yourself. You're too much of a talent. You know how Hanson is working for a recording date. He almost has something lined up. You going to blow your chances?"

"To hell with Hanson! To hell with it all!"

Don looked at him for a long while, not saying anything; then he pulled out his wallet and took out several bills.

"Here!" he said, laying down a half a dozen twenties on the table. "That should take care of the drinks, and enough to get you loaded and keep you that way! I'm going back to bed!"

He stood and then walked out without another word.

Bill didn't care. It didn't make any difference in the world to him. He just stared at the bills and then finally looked up, motioning toward the bartender. "Give me about five double shots all in a row!"

Drink, drink, my happy laddies!

Bitterly!

Drink and know of sin!

That was for sure!

Drink to the sexy Ladies.

Wherever they might be.

That you're 'bout to win!

He sat there, slowly sipping one drink after another. The world hazed, becoming a dizziness spinning around his head.

Drunk, drunk us happy laddies.
Drunk, knee-deep in play!
Drunk with a sexy Lady,
That we're 'bout to lay!

Where, oh, where was Laura Jones?
Gone to her grave.
Where is her beauty, now?
Gone for a long day…

Forever and ever. Gone, her beauty and charm,
gone beyond his gentle touch. Gone, never to return.
Dead, lying in her grave, no more to play!
He was aware of a man shaking him and he looked up at a fuzzy face.

"Say, buddy. It's four in the morning. You better get on home!"

He didn't say anything, but slowly staggered to

his feet. For a long time he had the feeling of walking through a world gone mad, one that wouldn't stop weaving in and out of shape before his eyes. One that twisted and pulled apart, only to gently distort back together, out of shape.

Suddenly everything was spinning, circling around him. He heard voices, but couldn't make out what they were saying. Then he fell forward and felt the impact of something hard hit his face. As he lay in the darkness that had welled around him he felt a gentle hand caress his forehead. He opened his eyes, but couldn't see anything. But a voice said in his ear:

"I'm here, my darling, I'm here, in the blackness of your mind. Take me in your arms of love. Carry me high on its wings to the summit of love's own union!"

He felt a silken form press gently to him. It was nude and giving and soft, Lips crushed to his and he folded his arms around the air He could feel her touching him and hear her voice and breathing in his ear, but his arms circled thin air.

"No. No, my darling. You cannot caress me anymore; you cannot hold me anymore. But let me kiss, let me caress, let me soothe your tired mind and soul. Oh, hold me in your heart keep me dear and tenderly in your mind's eye!"

"Oh, yes. Yes!" he sobbed out. *"Yes, yes!"*

His eyes opened and were blinded by a strong light that shined across them from a window. He was looking up at a ceiling, white and clean.

For a moment he couldn't understand what had happened, or where he was. A rawness was in his throat. His tongue was dry and thick. His body

67

seemed to ache, numbly.

He lay there, not moving, for a long time, not thinking, only aware that he was lying in a bed, somewhere in the living, sober world, and didn't understand how he had gotten there.

* * * * * * *

The doctor came up to Terry, where she was half sleeping in the waiting room. "You can see him now, if you want to."

Terry felt startled. She was tired, but suddenly a burst of energy surged through her. She'd been in a state of utter emotional exhausted confusion ever since Don had called her. That was yesterday when he got the report from Hanson, who had said Bill Carter had been picked up on a drunk charge.

Terry met Don in the lobby of the hotel where the unmarried members of the combo had been staying for the last few months. The two of them went in his car to the police station.

It took two hours to pay Bill's fine and have him transferred to a hospital.

"What's that for?" she had questioned the bass man when he'd told her what he had arranged.

"That's where he belongs. Maybe that will clear up his brain. We have to get him in shape as soon as possible. Maybe the shock of waking in the hospital will jolt him maybe not. Anyway he'll be in a place where they can give him some medical help. Dope him up, maybe. I don't know. Dry him out! But it sounded like the best thing to do!"

Bill was out like a light all the way to the hospital. He was put in a private room and then Don went home. Terry stayed to be there when he awakened. She had the feeling that he might need a friend

She waited all through the morning and the afternoon.

That's when the doctor appeared to say that Bill was awake now.

Chapter Seven

Bill looked into the face of Terry Anson, who was leaning fairly close to his. She was sitting on a chair, next to the bed. Her face tried to smile bravely, but there was a cloud of concern in her dark eyes.

"How long do you plan on keeping me here?" he demanded, bitterly. It had only been a couple of hours since he'd regained consciousness. He'd tried to get answers from the hospital personnel, but it hadn't done any good; they were tightlipped.

"Look, honey, I don't know. I just heard that you'd been picked up on a drunk charge and they decided it best that you be put in the hospital for a bit. You'd been hurt a little on the face and they wanted to look into that. Then they called Don, and he posted bail, but asked them to put you here. I came right down the moment I heard."

"What the hell does Don have to say about me?" he demanded, sitting up and looking angrily at Terry's pretty little face.

"He's worried. And so am I. All the boys are concerned. And you have—"

"Sure. Everybody is worried about the..." he let the thought sag, fading off, unfinished. It had been a nasty remark that he had almost made, and even in his emotionally tormented state, he couldn't bring himself to blast his friends too much; or unjustly.

He stared at Terry for a long while, taking in her rounded, dark features. She had an oval face, framed in short black hair. Her lips were pouty and full, little dimples in the corners. When she smiled her face became almost rounded, as her cheeks puffed out. She was a pretty bundle of sex, with a figure that bounced, from her full breasts to the rounded curving form of her buttocks. She had on a tight fitting suit, personally tailored for her figure to show off every sexy curve.

His mind's eye rejected her image for a moment and Laura's thinner form appeared over hers. Only for a second did he let himself look at that picture, forcing himself to focus back on Terry.

"I want to get the hell out of here!" he told her, firmly.

"I'll see what I can do," she commented, starting to stand. "But I don't know anything about this, honey. Be back in a while."

He sat there thinking about what he was going to do with his life; life without Laura, and he couldn't come up with any answer that made for a happy or useful seeming future. He just wanted to escape in a bottle. Fold the world around him until all awareness had faded out. Until he couldn't think through the blindness of being drunk. He simply wanted to "stop the world and get off!"

Terry returned with a doctor who stepped to the bedside, looked down at Bill and then smiled. "Well, let's see how you are!"

In a few minutes the man had taken his blood

pressure, pulse, and listened to his heart. Then standing he sighed. "You can go any time you wish. Your friend took care of everything…a Don Jenson. Last night when you were brought here. He was the one who asked that you be signed in."

"Thanks!" Bill said in a biting voice, sliding out of bed. Then he realized that he wasn't dressed and looked toward Terry who was smiling with a sharp, amused look in her eyes.

Let her look all she wants to!

He ignored her and stood. There were hospital bed clothing on him and she couldn't see much and it didn't really make any difference.

Give the girl a thrill!

Suddenly he was aware of an unconscious conclusion that he had made: he was going to let Terry see him with less on than he now had. He was going to give her what she'd been trying to get for a long time.

Better her than the tramps he'd apparently been bedding.

"I guess we better leave while Mr. Carter gets dressed," the doctor laughed.

"Oh, I don't mind!" Bill said.

"Neither to I, honey!" she laughed, sweeping his body with flashing eyes.

He was tempted to open the robe and flash her a real view of what she so obviously wanted to see. But he held back that impulse.

A moment later Bill was in the small room by himself. It only took a few seconds to find his clothing in the small closet, and he quickly pulled them on.

Finally he stepped out of the room and over to

the nurse's desk where Terry was waiting.

"Anything else I have to do?" he asked one of the nurses.

"Just sign this form, that's all. Then you can go." He took the pen she offered and signed, then turned and took Terry's hand in his, leading her out of the hospital.

She gave him a surprised look as he took hold of her fingers and squeezed slightly. It was the first time that he had actually done anything even that intimate with her. Her fingers were amazingly soft and warm, very sensual.

"Some change in you?" she commented dryly when they were outside.

"Don't expect too much!"

"I won't. Promise!"

"Want to split, together?"

"We are together, aren't we?" she pointed out lightly. "What to make something out of it!"

"You have some money?" he asked, looking her straight in the eyes.

"Oh, that's it, then!"

"What?"

"You just want me for my money!" she giggled.

"No, that's not it! I'm flat, right now. But in the bank there's plenty. Loan me a twenty or so and I'll pay you later when I get to the bank. Right now I want to take you out for a drink."

"What makes you think I want to go out with you?" she teased.

"Don't play games, Terry!" he told her in a hard, serious and demanding voice. "Either you're in or you're out!"

"I think you got that backwards!"

"What?"

"That's my line, I think?"

"What?"

"You're either…in…or out!" She smiled, evilly.

"Well, make up your mind!"

She nodded and laughed. "I'm in-*terested!* You should know that!" She took hold of his arm and the two of them walked down the street.

"I know you've been interested for a long time," he told her in an even voice. "So it's cash in time, I suppose!"

"So, I haven't hid it. Shame on me!"

"So, stop complaining and cash in!" he said, blank faced. He really couldn't care less, but if he was going to take a ride with the girl he didn't want any foolish games getting in the way. And he didn't want to be with some stranger who couldn't be trusted. If he had to screw around with a female body, let it be Terry. She could be taken for fun and games. A free-spirited ride into the land of total escape.

"Are you sure?" she asked, "This is what you want?"

"Terry. I'll say it once. And that's it. I don't want to think. I don't want to feel anything except out of it. I'd rather be with a friend than a stranger. Nothing more!"

She considered that seriously for a moment as they stood outside a bar. "You don't give any roses to a lady."

"I'm not in the moon for romantic shit!" he snapped, furiously.

She nodded, "I suppose not."

"Damned right."

"Come on, I'm your friendly party girl, if that's what you need!"

They stepped into a cocktail lounge and settled in a booth in a dim corner. When the waitress came he ordered two double martinis and then turned his attention to Terry. "Well, it's taken a long time but here we are." Then he added, bitterly, "You get what you wanted."

"What's that?"

"Me, I suppose. Isn't that want you've been after for some time?" He couldn't keep the angry emotion out of his voice. It wasn't at her so much as at the situation.

"That's nasty!" Terry observed. "Makes me sound terrible. I never touched you! Never made any serious pass. That's not fair."

"Life isn't fair! Shit on it!" he exploded a little loud. "And either you wanna take me on my terms or you can just walk out right now!"

She was silent for a few minutes, then taking a deep breath, said: "So…we do it your way."

"I figured as much!" he announced rather flatly.

"You're sure cocky! What made you think I'd jump at your command?" she asked, her eyes flashing slightly.

"Because that's you," he assured her, reaching out for her hands. But she pulled them off the small table and down to her lap. There was an edge of annoyance in her eyes.

"I don't know what kind of woman you think I am, Bill, but don't get too fancy an idea about me!"

"And what does that mean?"

"Anything you want it to mean, I guess!"

He sat there, looking carefully at Terry, aware

75

that she was slightly nervous under his gaze. Her eyes didn't meet his, but kept shifting away.

The drinks came and he downed a third of his in one gulp. It tasted good. Good and strong. He had needed a drink.

Terry only sipped her cocktail.

They didn't speak to each other for a long time, but sat there in silence.

"What are you going to do about the gig, honey?" Terry finally asked, taking another sip of her martini.

"Nothing!"

"Nothing?" she exploded, almost angrily, looking sharply at him. "You can't do that to the boys!"

"I'm doing it. I'm out! That's the end. I don't want anything to do with that kind of jazz anymore."

"You can't stop living!" she countered.

"Who said anything about stopping that?"

"But you—"

"Look, Terry, let's cut the chatter about the gig. I don't want to blow any more of that kind of music talk! Got that?"

She shrugged and then asked: "Then what do you want to talk about?"

"Nothing! Just get loaded and then let matters fuck themselves."

She stared at Bill for a long time without saying anything, biting her lower lip nervously. She seemed to make up her mind about something. "Okay, Bill, if that's the way you want."

There was bitterness in her words, but also something that sounded like regret and hopelessness combined.

"That's my girl!" he snapped.

A hurt expression crossed her face. "Wish it was so," she almost whispered.

"What?"

"Nothing."

Suddenly she grabbed her martini and downed it in one gulp.

"If that's what you want, then let's get on with the party!" she saluted with her glass. But even though her words and actions were light and gay he detected a note of sadness in her voice. But he decided to ignore it. Terry had made up her mind to stick it out with him for the next few hours at least and she seemed to think the best way was to keep up with him, martini-wise.

Bill smiled and then turned and called for the cocktail girl. He ordered another round and it came in a few minutes. Neither of them said much after that. There were slight smiles exchanged, but every time she smiled he had the feeling it was forced and thought he saw a little sadness in her eyes when she looked at him.

Finally they were working on their fourth martini and at last he saw that she was beginning to get high. That was the sign he had been waiting for. Once he got Terry high enough it wouldn't matter how she had felt sober, she'd be really in the mood for anything. Once high, Terry just wanted to party; that much he knew, because he'd seen her near drunk enough times in the past.

Her hands reached for his, as she smiled.

"So you want to run away and hide, well you came to the joy-girl herself!" she said, lightly, squeezing his fingers. "I'll hide away with you, for as long as you need me."

"Sure…why not?" was his only bitter comment. He really didn't care much, actually. Only that it would be safer with Terry than some nameless pickup.

"Another drink," he ordered, and let his mind float away.

His long "weekend" was starting again.

Bill didn't remember leaving the cocktail lounge with Terry, or going to the hotel room, or seducing her. He woke up in bed, an aching pain in his head. He felt, more than anything, a body next to him in bed. He knew it was Terry. For a moment annoyance teased him: he didn't remember having sex with Terry. They'd been in a bar together; everything else was a blackout. Sighing, he looked around the room.

It was a classy place he'd landed in this time. But that must have been Terry's influence. Slowly getting up, he walked to the stand on the other side of the room and picked up the hotel phone. A moment later he had the operator on the line.

"Send up some booze!" he said.

"What do you want?" the voice asked.

"I don't give a goddam! A bottle of whiskey."

"Say, how about some food?" Terry's sleepy voice interrupted him from across the room.

He looked toward her. She was sitting up in bed, her large, bouncy breasts exposed over the top of the covers. Her eyes were squinting against the morning light that shined through the open window. Her face had the look of puffy sleep.

"An order of ham and eggs, too," he demanded over the receiver. "And make it fast with the booze!"

Then he hung up, stepped over to the bed and sat down on the edge of it, looking at Terry. He tried to smile, but he didn't feel that it came off. His eyes looked at her full, brimming breasts.

It was the first time he was aware of seeing them naked. He looked carefully, realizing he'd probably smothered himself against their blooming fullness, feasted on the ripe, rosy nipples. She was lush and better than he'd imagined. In fact, staring at her, he realized he'd never really had a serious fantasy about her, not even creating a mental picture of what she might be in the stark.

Now all he had to do was look and then take the all of her into his arms. At least she was great to look at, certainly better than the faceless objects he'd picked up a few days back. Literally fantastically better!

A shutter rushed over him.

"What's wrong?" she asked.

"Nothing that you can't help fit," he muttered, almost convinced. It really didn't matter. All he needed was to dive in and drown.

"Like what you see?" She smiled as she noticed the direction of his gaze.

"Just noticing what I must have been enjoying..."

"You really were something last night. Just wild something super!"

"I don't remember."

"What a shame."

"Well, maybe you'll help me forget again!"

"Why forget?" she offered, stretching, causing her breasts to swell. Then she said in a low voice that was thick with morning sleep: "I take it you approve?"

Her arms reached out for him. "Come here, love and enjoy them!"

Chapter Eight

For a second he didn't quite know what she was talking about, and then it suddenly sank in. "You have one pair of beauts!" he commented dryly.

"Well, you don't have to be so bored about it. You sure went wild with them last night!" She smiled broadly this time and extended a hand out to his. Gripping his fingers tightly, she leaned forward, parting her lips. He met them with his own.

The touch was subtle but sensual. She had soft feeling lips that gave under the gentlest pressure. They were warm and moist.

She sighed and leaned back. "Even drunk you were not so bad. Really, not so bad at all!" she said half to herself and half to him, looking at the far wall for a moment before returning her eyes to his. She smiled slightly. "You were really smashed!"

"I guess so, I don't remember anything!"

She laughed at that. "Boy! That's really a hoot. You should have seen yourself."

"So?" he commented humorlessly. He couldn't really have cared less. He wanted a drink, and bad. He needed something to dull awareness and reality. To keep out of focus, so that he couldn't think about Laura.

A deep, heavy sigh shook through him at the thought of Laura. Then he forced his attention on the pointed centers of Terry's lovely breasts.

He stared at her for a long time, examining in detail every fraction of her nipples, finding a fascination in looking at them. They were rosy and very beautiful.

Rosy Cherries,
Ripe and ready,
Not like dark, hard berries,
But nipples, erect and steady!

"You enjoying yourself?" she asked abruptly, a light touch of humor in her voice.

He just smiled and then looked up at her face. Those eyes were bright and shining, and there was a slight glaze to them. She was drunk more with desire than booze; and her face was flushed.

Her lips pursed in a kiss and then spread into a smile. "I take it you like my breasts?"

"So?"

"You've been staring at them...as if devouring them."

Breasts ready to be had.

Full spheres waiting for play! And lips wanting to say, Take me in your arms today! Focus on them and nothing more!

"You got boobs! For sure!"

"God, Bill, you make a girl feel so wanted!" It was lightly said, but an undercurrent of something else edged the words slightly dull.

"You're hardly unattractive," he said.

"Thanks for small compliments!" she offered,

flatly.

Bill was now leaning towards her and brushed a light finger on her breasts. She tensed under the touch and her eyes half closed.

He sat there, just looking at her reaction for a long while, not really feeling anything except the dry bitterness that she wasn't Laura.

The dead woman's body calls,
Take me in your arms of love,
And we will spread our wings,
To the high skies above!

Terry cupped her hands under her breasts, like platters in offering: "Take them, they're all yours."

He reached out, pulling her close and feeling her breasts press against the nakedness of his chest. They were soft and yielding, supple and warm; pulsing with life and passion. Her lips sought his and for a long moment their tongues moved together in fast, rapid rhythm.

He felt a heat of angry desperation flood over him, pulling his muscles into tight steel until she was crushed in the viselike embrace of his arms. She squirmed and then came up for air.

"God, you're better than last night," she half sobbed in his ear.

He didn't care about that; he didn't want to care about anything right then. Caring hurt and what he needed was "escape"—which her body now so willingly offered.

"You...don't know how long...I've wanted you!" she whispered in his ear, working her tongue along the lobe.

He slowly moved her down, crosswise on the bed, pushing the covers away from her body until he could blend his to hers.

She strained against him, moaning slightly. Then their lips met, trembling and open, warm and moist. He felt her tongue stab past his teeth and settle there, tasting in the sensation of him, and then it started exploring carefully.

There was a knock on the door.

For a moment they froze.

"Bellboy with your order," a voice called out to them.

"Damn! Be right there!" he heard his own voice curse. Then slowly, reluctantly, he moved from Terry and stood.

"Cover yourself," he savagely growled, walking to the chair where his pants were neatly folded. He put them on, slipped into his shirt, then walked to the door and flung it open.

The bellboy walked in with the tray and set it down on the dresser, then turned for his tip. Bill looked toward Terry and she indicated her purse with a pointing finger. He picked it up from the floor and opened it. After a moment of searching he found a dollar bill and handed it to the man.

The bellboy looked at him sharply, and he searched out another dollar and handed it to the man. The guy left, closing the door after him.

Terry quickly uncovered herself and stepped out of bed.

The sight of her moving across the small room, her rounded, full hips jerking with every step, charged an electric reaction through Bill. He just devoured her with his eyes, taking in every inch of her body as it moved. It had an animal catlike action about it.

She smiled and went to the food on the tray.

"You sure you don't want anything?" she asked once she'd set things up so that she could eat at the small desk in the corner of the room.

"You kidding?" He moved to her and reached his arms around her body so that his hands sank into the fullness of her breasts. "I'll feast on them!"

"Stop that!" she ordered in a much too nervous voice. "Let me eat first!"

He sighed and then reached for the bottle the bellboy had brought up. He opened the top and raised it to his mouth.

"Hey! Don't get drunk on me!" she yelled, anxiously. "I want to know what s like when you're sober!"

"Forget it, baby. I'll be sober! I need something!"

"I want you to remember it, this time. To know how I feel all wrapped up around you like a tight fitting blanket on a hot winter night."

"That's an oxymoron!" he actually laughed.

"Oh? Then, I suppose…let's see, honey…a soft warm embrace on a cold winter night? To keep you from freezing it all away."

She looked down, meaningfully. Grinning. "You sure get big with you're excited!"

"Well you're an exciting woman." It was an automatic verbal retort.

Her expression was sad as she glanced up at him. Then after a moment she returned her attention to the food.

He sat on the bed, watching her eat. Watching

her he could see just a little of her back and the large and complete shape of her pointed breast. Her arm rose with each bite she took and her breasts went tense and then relaxed, bobbing slightly with every action her arm made. He gulped on the bottle again, feeling the whiskey burn down his throat and then settle in his stomach. It was like warm, soothing fingers spreading through his system and then finally upward to his brain. He felt the light sensation of his head becoming fuller and then take on the feel of floating, as he took a third large gulp of whiskey.

His eyes never left the action of Terry's breasts. Finally he stood and moved to her, reaching a hand under the large curve of her bust.

She jumped as if shocked, then turned and looked at him.

"What are you trying to do?" she murmured, a sparkle in her eyes.

"You guess!" he demanded, pressing harder.

"Hey!" she cried," that hurts!"

"I thought you would like it!" he laughed, leaning over and kissing her throat. The silken skin seemed to tremble under his lips.

"Aren't you going to let me eat in peace?" she complained.

He ignored the remark, sliding his other hand around her body so that it sunk into the swell of her breast on that side.

"Damn it all, leave me alone!" she cried, a laugh breaking from her lips.

"Why?" he asked, fondling the fullness of her, and running his lips up to her ear so that he could work the lobe between them. "Does that bother

86

you?"

A light murmur sighed from her, and she half closed her eyes.

He slid one hand down under the curve of her breast and then along the flatness of her stomach.

"That's enough!" she cried firmly, but didn't do anything to stop him.

He bit his teeth into her ear lobe and she suddenly twisted in his arms, her lips desperately seeking his, her hands clawing at the back of his head. Their tongues met, and then suddenly he pulled her up into his arms and took her over to the bed, laid her down, and slipped alongside of her.

She moaned loudly as he ran his fingers, caressingly, along her body. And then her hands clawed at his, digging them deeper and savagely into her breasts. Her body squirmed and then she turned toward him. Finally the overwhelming desire blended them into one unified movement. He was aware of the tightness of her hot flesh gripping him, and her thighs seemed like an embracing vice, locking him in place. There was little tenderness, only a savage taking, two animals in heat, demanding total use of one another until they lay exhausted on the bed, half-conscious.

She was the first to stir, but it took several minutes before she stood from the bed. A little later she sat at the table and finished her meal.

Before Terry was finished eating, Bill had reached for the bottle, and gulped whiskey, only stopping long enough to let the burn settle in his stomach and to judge the effect it would have on him.

She stood and turned to look at him.

"What are you doing?" she snapped, almost angrily. "You can't get yourself drunk again!"

"Oh yeah?" he cried back, waving the bottle in the air.

She stared at him for a long time, not saying anything, only her lips compressed in an expression of resigned annoyance. Finally she relaxed and sighed, as if she had decided the best way to keep him was to keep him happy. She moved to the bed and seemed to force a smile: "Come on, honey, don't drink it all yourself. I want a little, too!"

He handed her the bottle, his hand weaving slightly from the effects of the liquor. His head was already spinning again in that sea of swirling dizziness.

"Drink, Drink, my happy shaddies!" he shouted, laughing.

"Shrink, Shrink and know of shin!
"Sink, to the sheckies, Ladies,
"That shure out to shin!"

"Shay, you know, baby," he whispered, leaning toward Terry and sinking his face into the fullness of her breasts, "Shu have one shell of a hare of cherries!" he cried sitting up and looking her full in the eyes. But she was weaving in front of his eyes. "Shay still!" he shouted at her, reaching out and grabbing hold of he head He pulled the head against his. Finally he managed to find her lips, but couldn't see her.

He felt he lips open and then moved his tongue past her teeth. She clamped her mouth around it, hungrily working it with her own tongue.

He just sat there letting her do all the work.

Drunk, drunk us happy laddies,
Drunk, knee-deep in play!
Drunk with the sexy Lady.
That we're 'bout to lay...

* * * * * * *

The room was dark. He could hear heavy breathing and it wasn't for a long time that he realized that it was his own. Dimly he remembered making love to Terry Anson. It was a dull, distant memory of flesh, sensation, nothing more. He reached out an arm for her.

It met empty bed.

He turned, startled.

Terry wasn't in the bed. Where was she?

He looked around the room, but it was too dark to see very clearly, yet he guessed she wasn't there. He couldn't hear a sound.

"Terry! You there?" he called out, anyway.

No answer.

He forced himself to lie back and try to relax. Maybe she had only gone out for a little while. He might as well sleep.

Awareness slipped away.

He awoke again.

The sun was shining through the window and he sat slowly up in bed. His guts were aching and his head had a painful band around it.

The first thing he noticed was that Terry wasn't in the room. The second thing was that her clothes weren't in the room, either.

He sighed and slowly moved out of bed and then across to the bath room. The face that looked

89

back at him in the mirror was covered with a week-old beard. It was puffy and blurry eyed. He stared at the image and could hardly recognize it as a reflection of himself. Then finally he took a deep breath and started for the shower. First he would have to clean himself and then go down and have something to eat. Get a shave and then have a few drinks; the first for the day. After that maybe he'd get himself some money from the bank. He would need it. He had already forgotten all about Terry.

Twenty minutes later he was walking across the hotel lobby.

"Mister Carter?" a voice called to him from the desk. He turned and looked. "You Mister Carter?" the clerk asked.

He nodded and stepped over to the counter. "The lady described what you looked like and said that if I saw you I was supposed to give you this envelope."

Bill took it and opened it. There was a note and about thirty dollars in bills. He looked at the note and read:

> *"Dear Bill,*
>
> *"Even I don't want you this way. The enclosed cash will is all I had. When you snap out of it, you know where to find me,*
>
> *Love,*
>
> *"Terry."*

He didn't feel anything. The only thing that really mattered was the money.

"What's the bill here?" he asked.

"The lady paid it up for a week in advance. By check," the man told him.

Bill just nodded and then walked away toward the coffee shop at the other side of the lobby, pocketing the money, without a second thought about the woman who had given it to him. As far as he was concerned she didn't matter in the least. He could find some other broad to screw when he wanted one!

First he would eat. Get a shave. Have some drinks. Go to his bank and get some money. Then lights out!

* * * * * * *

Don Jenson slowly stepped into his hotel room, feeling his whole mind and body about to explode under the nervous tension of the last few days.

A blowup had flared between him and Hanson at the club that evening after the last set. The agent had been back stage when he stepped behind the small curtain.

"Okay, what's with this Carter guy?" the man had demanded, chewing on his cigar butt. He was a visual satire of the agent, PR man.

"I don't know anything more than you do, man."

"We have to get him in line on this!"

"I don't even know where he is!" Don snapped, angrily. He'd been being pushed from all sides, and when Terry had gone to Bill there had been a

BLUES FOR A DEAD LOVER, BY CHARLES NUETZEL

strange feeling of unrest; a feeling that he didn't like.

"Look, he's the headliner, how long do you think I can keep the management of this dive off my back? Don't like them clawing at me that way! How long?"

"Until Bill comes out of it. He's gone off on an escape-bender. You can't blame him. There isn't anything that we can do about it!"

"Okay! Okay. You just do what you can. That recording bit is off for the season!"

"Another will come along!" Don told the man, taking a deep tired breath.

"Sure! But it made me look like a monkey. I don't like being made a monkey out of! No way!"

"Oh, look here, man. Don't you have any heart? This guy had seen hell—and that's a big blow! If he isn't dead somewhere. I'm worry. But…chances are he's safe and sound in some hotel, drunk with… never mind that."

"Screwing some broad, no doubt. Some tragic lover he is! One dies and he's off fucking some broad!"

"Christ, man. Have a heart! You think it's fun for him?"

"I don't like men that go to pieces over a dumb broad! And especially when it gets in my way!" Hanson snapped, turning and leaving.

Don had gone to his room.

He felt exhausted as he flopped down on the small bed. The unsettling feelings that had been running through him about Terry and Bill were a little frightening.

There was that horrible gnawing in his guts that

told him that he'd let himself get too interested in Terry. How it had happened he didn't know. The only thing that mattered was he was too hot for Terry in too many ways.

The woman wasn't the kind to easily ignore.

And when she sang a song it could or near orgasm time, once she turned the sex on full blast. She caused a lyric to become a love-fest. When she did "Do It Again" a guy wanted to do just that. She made words sound so hot and intimate, so hungrily demanding that every man within hearing distance, who was paying attention, was driven raw with desire. And Terry knew just how to lean over, just enough, to show off the full valley between her breasts, teasingly accenting every word. "Please, do it again," caused a man to shiver with desire to do it again and again every time she sang those words. And every time she said them her voice caressed hotter and hungrier around the lyrics.

Her style with the mike was almost risqué, without being vulgar. She used that instrument as not only a volume control, but as a kind of sensual symbol which her lips almost touched, almost parted around, almost fed on.

Once she'd told him: "I use that thing like it is a man's more proud possession and try to imply anything he wants to imagine—but to be truthful, I learned early to use it as a way to control the intimacy of my voice, to whisper words that shouldn't be shouted. How can you scream *I love you* and have them believe you? I want them to lust for me. I want my songs to reach deep into their very being, to focus on my whole…message. A woman in love, a woman wanting her man, a woman who will whisper sweet hot nothings into her lover's ears. Not shout them. So the mike, to me, is an instrument of intimacy, a means to truly whisper into a man's ears all the promises of love. And, well, I'm a gonna make it look like something else, if the man's willing to imagine!" And when she said that last, her eyes sparkled warm and almost lovingly. "My lips appear to kiss the mike, breathing into it, parting slightly. Oh, the images men confess to having when I do that. I want them to imagine I'm right there, breathing on them, I want them to feel me in the most—well, it sure gives a girl a charge, that does for sure!"

She had laughed at that, very throatily. But the look in her eyes had said it all. She was turned on as much as she wanted to turn on an audience.

And she had turned him on fully in the telling. Terry was a complicated woman, and in some way very much what she appeared on stage to be: a hot chick out to embrace all takers. Yet there was another element that was surprising: she truly cared about people. And especially about Bill Carter. Everybody knew that.

And every man who knew her had a hard on for Terry.

And some, like himself, a bit more than that.

He finally relaxed, blanking his mind out and then falling into restful sleep.

He was awakened by the phone ringing.

Groggily he sat up in bed and reached for the phone. "Hello?"

"Don! This is Terry, I have to see you!"

Chapter Nine

Terry looked across at Don with a worried expression in her eyes. All he could think of was how lovely and lonely and confused and hurt she looked.

"I don't know what to do," she told him, starting to idly finger the rim of her coffee cup.

"What any of us can do," she added grimly.

"I know, Terry, I tried. But you know Bill. The thing we have to worry about is keeping the group together so when he snaps out of it..."

"If there was just something that we could do!" Terry cried out in desperation.

"He has to bat his own head in. It'll take time, but he'll come out of it. The other night, when I picked him up...well, it was just impossible."

"I thought that maybe...I'd be a help," Terry choked, softly. "He's horrid. In terrible condition. He simply doesn't care about anything...but that... Laura woman!"

Don shrugged, knowing the pain Terry much be feeling. She was in a completed fix between normal human desire and normal human sadness about the death of another person.

"I feel terrible," Terry continued, talking rapidly, "about Laura, of course. But I...well wasn't in love with her. She…well…once she was there, I had no way to hook Bill even into a casual thing. I feel terrible about…well…feeling good about a chance to have him…. Oh, Don, I'm horrid!"

Her voice choked to silence.

"Nothing wrong about how you feel, Terry," he told her gently. "We all have our burdens. We all need something. And we're all pretty damned self-centered, egocentric and don't like the competition! And Laura was that, for you!"

Don was thinking how Bill was his competition, in a way. He could fully relate to Terry's feelings. But he could hardly tell her the truth about his own. Not right now; maybe never.

"Oh, God, Don, I'm conflicted. And he was horrid! Really! I feel terribly sorry for him. I know the pain he's feeling. But quite frankly I can't feel it, too. I only keep thinking, now I have my chance! And that's disgusting. What's wrong with me?'

"Nothing, nothing at all, Terry!"

Something about the way he said that seemed to catch her attention. Her eyes snapped to his for a moment, then drifted away. "I'm sorry."

The way she said that was vague. He wasn't sure what she meant by it, so he said: "Don't blame yourself."

"Oh, I'm not that foolish, Don!" she exclaimed, looking into the man's eyes.

"You love him a lot, don't you?" Don asked, folding his hand over hers, tenderly.

She just nodded, sad-eyed. "I think so. Just not the way he is right now. Damn Laura, anyway!"

That was, for sure, a conflicted statement, and her voice held all the emotion of angry fury, jeal-

ousy and love all mixed together with terrible personal pain.

They didn't say anything for a long while, then
Don finally stated: "Hanson wants to see Bill. He's
been on my neck and I've stalled him. When you
phoned from the hotel room, that first evening you
were with him, Hanson was at the club then, and I'd
been talking to him. It was a job to put him off."

"What's going to happen?" she asked, her voice
heavy with worry.

"The group's going to split up if we don't get
Billy back into shape. You left him at the hotel...bombed out of his mind?"

"Out like a light. I waited until I was sure then
left. It's disgusting what's happening to him!" she
bitterly snapped. "Even if you like or love a guy—
nobody can take much of the—"

"I know!" Don sighed, tiredly. "Can I go there
and see him?"

"Why not?"

"I mean: think he'll listen?"

"Hell, no!'

"What if I took Hanson?"

She shrugged. "Look, if I didn't do any good—"

"You just added to it. All he wants is booze and
women."

"I guess you're right. You make it sound so
cheap. Make me sound like...well, never mind that!
I probably am! Free spirit and all that crap! Men
don't know what a girl goes through to get ahead in
this business. And a man in my position would be
considered some great stud, admired by all. A girl is
just called a slut and tramp. She gets lonely at
nights, she hurts and has needs. And she's supposed

to be some virginal child in a chastity belt or something. And I might look like Ms. Wonder Woman, Love Thrill of the night, but I've had my chunk of pain and losses, and I know what it feels like to be spit on and looked down on and consider...oh forget it."

"Terry, don't do that to yourself."

"Why not? It's the truth. Men have one standard for themselves and another for us woman. They don't even call us that. Chicks, girls, skirts, hot lays, and you name it and I've heard it."

"And what do you girls call us?"

"You don't want to hear that, my friend." She almost laughed at that.

"Now you've got my interest up."

"The way woman talk in private, well, is private. You'd be shocked at what some say."

"I doubt it. I've known a few who say it pretty raw and crude."

"I suppose."

He wanted to pull her into his arms, tenderly comfort her. But instead simply sat there staring and wanting and fighting down those feelings, bottling them up.

"What can a girl do?" she asked suddenly, very serious. "I tried the jumping in bed routine, keeping a close eye on him, not wanting him to be alone in his drunken binge. But that didn't work. I want to be supportive, but don't know how. I've wanted him for so long, Don. What can I do?"

"His life is broken. You can't fix it for him," Don announced without emotion. "I went through it once. Some broad left me hanging; took all she could from me, and then skipped. So I was out on the bender for one hell of a long time. Drink. Women. The drinking passes in a few weeks or months, but not the bitter taste and the painful hurt. You go through life after that just existing. It took over two years to blast my way out of feeling sorry for myself. Then I met you!"

He broke off, suddenly, realizing he'd said too much.

Terry looked sharply at him. Her eyes frowned. "I'm sorry. I never knew!"

"Forget it," Don said, looking down at his hands.

They sat in silence for a long while, neither looking at the other, then finally Don started to slide out of the booth. "I'll go call Hanson and then go over to the hotel and see Bill. Maybe between the two of us we can push a little sense into his brain!"

* * * * * * *

As Terry stood and walked out with him, then into the lobby towards her hotel room, she felt somewhat off-balance by Don's blurted confession. Up until that point, she had never thought much about the man, other than as a friend. Oh, she'd realized he had the normal male interest in her body, but that was normal. They flirted at times, but it was seemingly harmless stuff. Now she saw it somewhat differently and hated having strung him along in that manner. Even if innocently. She had a lot of thinking to do. A lot of organizing of her thoughts about herself and Bill, and the way she really felt about him.

Right from the start she'd been attracted to the

man. They had flirted a bit, right off, which was meaningless. She flirted with any man alive. It was a wonderful game; not a cock tease. Mutual flattery and verbal fun, mentally challenging to get very close to the line, without going over it, unless both parties involved wanted that. She knew exactly how far to take a flirt without being truly seductive. With Bill she'd played it safe and careful, finding out how things stood. After all he was the lead man. It could be a problem getting too intimate with the boss. On the other hand, it was necessary to let him know she thought they could have something together, if that's what he wanted.

And she'd planned that out very carefully one evening at a break between sets, deciding to use the cigarette gag she'd used from time to time.

"Honey," she'd said, back stage, "you're sure blowing great tonight."

"I guess so."

"Makes a girl just wonder."

"What?"

"Well, you know." She had looked up into his eyes, rather suggestively. "You're really hot tonight, aren't you?"

"You sure make that sound suggestive," he laughed.

"It was supposed to be," was her simple admission.

"Naughty lady! For shame!"

"No shame in it. When a girl feels flushed all over, what's she supposed to do? Just bat her eyes?" She batted her eyes, fluttering the lids as rapidly as possible. "Does that make you so hot you can't control yourself?"

100

"Honey, you're hot enough without the batting," he countered with a laugh, lighting a cigarette.

"Give me a puff?" she asked, taking his hand, pulling it towards her lips. He turned the fingers so she could take a sip of the cigarette. She made it sexual, caressing its filter with her lips. Then she drew deeply on it. Her eyes never left his, sparkling suggestively all the time.

A moment later he looked at the filter, now covered in lipstick. He chuckled, said: "Now you've messed it all up!"

"I thought you've find that sexy," she murmured, wanting to come in close and embrace him, but standing there, unmoving.

"Well, it's red all over," he observed.

"I could make you red all over, if you wanted me to. Now wouldn't that be nice?"

That bought a huge belly laugh from him. What might have happened after that was never given a chance to mature. Somebody came up and took Bill away. She didn't see him again until the break was over and they were on stage.

She made a couple of other flirtatious suggestions, that were meant to be more fully developed in bed, and might have, if there had simply been more time to develop things.

But before anything could happen, Laura Jones entered, and that was it for Bill. Until now. With Laura gone, as horrible as it sounded, she had her first break to follow though with those earlier seductive moves. This was her first real in with Bill, and she didn't really know if she'd done the right thing walking out on him. But it had been the only thing left to her. He didn't know what he was doing half the time, and that wasn't the kind of man she wanted. Yet she should be seeing this through with him. One way or another. Even if it did end up as a wash, this time she didn't plan on letting things end, unless totally explored. There was nothing worse than never exhausting all possibilities with a man. It had to be played out, finalized so that one could go on. Bill's relationship with Laura was finished, done with, and all he had to realize was how nothing he could do could change that. He would have to face that hard reality.

She wanted, desperately, to help him. She needed to be there for him. But not yet. It was too soon. The last couple of days had proven that. He had no room for new feelings; not until he'd closed the wound of his lost love. The gap in his soul was too fresh, the open sore too violently seething in its own fury. Emotional acid was burning his guts away. At this point it really wasn't her place to be anything more than ready to move in when he wanted her; he wasn't her man—yet! All she was to Bill was a tumble in bed and nothing more. She knew that. And didn't need him that way.

Stepping up to the elevator she pressed the button and waited. She needed some sleep and rest, and time to think. Maybe the next day she could figure things out, but right now she was exhausted, drained and couldn't really think.

* * * * * * *

Hanson looked over his big cigar at Don Jenson. "Okay, sweetheart, shoot!" he exclaimed, leaning forward and peering into the man's eyes.

102

Don shuffled in his chair. He didn't know quite how to tell the agent. Hanson was one of those guys who might just fly off and blow the whole works apart. All Hanson knew was that Billy Carter had disappeared and nothing more.

"Look, I know where Bill is!"

"What?" the agent exploded. "Take me to him."

* * * * * * *

Bill Carter was sitting in the barber's chair when Don and Hanson found him.

"Hi there, sweetheart!" Hanson greeted in a light, almost happy voice. "Missed you around!"

Bill opened his eyes and looked into the thick features of his agent. He frowned. "What are you doing here?"

Hanson looked hurt, his expression compressing his heavy cheeks and large lips. "What's wrong, Billy-boy? This is me, your friend and second father!"

"Go home, second father!" Bill said coldly. "I don't need you!"

Hanson stared blankly at him for a moment and then a broad, oily smile spread across his face, showing thick corn-type teeth. "Look, son, I heard about the raw deal you got! Terrible. Terrible."

"And it breaks you all up, right?"

"Hey," the man exploded, "you don't think I'm heartless, do you?"

"I sometimes wonder. Aren't all of you agent promoter types cold-blooded assholes?"

Don exploded: "Christ, Bill!"

Hanson snapped: "Oh, shut up, bass man! I'm

103

not insulted. You can't insult a cold-blooded ass-hole, now can you?"

Bill glanced at the man, shrugged. "I suppose not!"

"Look, sweetheart, we need to get some things worked out. It is serious."

"Quit conning me!" Bill almost snarled. "I'm not at all interested."

"You can't let your feelings run wild!" the man exclaimed. "Look, we've all been through this kind of thing. I'm human, I understand, really I do."

"Bullshit!"

"Come on, I know exactly what you're going through!"

"Crap!"

Bill looked toward Don standing next to the agent.

"Get this ass out of here!" he said.

Don ignored him.

"Look, sweetheart, you can't just stop! You can't turn yourself off!"

"Oh, shut up!"

The barber had stood stunned, listening to them talk, his face white with surprise and shock.

"Come on. Let's be friendly," Hanson said, showing no outward reaction to his client's insults.

Bill seemed to relax suddenly and then tiredly sighed. "Look, you guys, so you're trying to help. But don't you know when a buddy doesn't want help? I just want to be left alone to—"

"To pull the world of fantasy around you and not face reality?" Don asked, harshly.

"None of your damned business!"

"Look, sweetheart, we need you with the group.

Without you the—"

"Oh, crap! Don't hand me that. I'm not *that* big a name!"

"The manager of the club thinks so!" Hanson commented dryly.

"Sure! So what. He'll believe anything he needs to…to run his club. They're all little squirts trying to survive and they have to deal with your kind of crap. Split the group up for all I care. Do what you want with it. I'm through! Got me?"

"There're contracts!" Hanson remarked coolly.

"So? I'm not blowing with the group anymore. I just want to be left alone! Got me?"

Hanson's face reddened and his eyes flared.

"Okay, sweetheart. I'll lay it on the line: there's a lot of money and time invested in you. *My* money and *my* time! You be on the job tomorrow night! And that's an order!"

"You goddamned bastard!" Bill cried, doubling his fists, and swinging his arm back. "Go fuck yourself!"

Don jumped forward, desperately grabbing hold of Bill's wrist. "Stop!"

"Leave me!"

Hanson broke in, calmly: "Look, you either play for me starting tomorrow, or you don't work any gig in town! Got that! You be at work tomorrow!"

Hanson started to turn to leave when Bill finally struggled free of Don, shoving his friend to one side, he leaped toward the agent, swinging him around. His hands were on the other's shoulders.

"Look, you no good shit! Get this straight. You can blackball me all you want! I couldn't care a damn less!" he yelled into the man's face.

"Get your hands off me!" Hanson ordered. Bill's hands slid to his side and the agent glared at him. "You're going to be sorry!" He turned to Don. "You headline the group from now on. Billy Carter here is finished with me and with every other agent in country. He doesn't want to blow trumpet, so let it be. He won't ever blow anything except a balloon!"

"Say, you can't do that!" Don objected. "He's not himself!"

Hanson looked coldly at the bass player. "Say another word! Just another one! There are other bass players!"

Hanson turned and walked out, not looking back. Don twisted toward Bill.

"Now what did that all prove?" he demanded, angrily.

Bill didn't answer him, he just sat in the chair, staring right through his friend. He didn't even give any indication that he saw the other man.

Don stood there for a moment and then stomped out.

* * * * * * *

The next morning Terry had made up her mind about herself and Bill.

If she really loved the man, there was only one thing that she could do: try to help him in any possible way. Even if he wasn't interested in her as a person at this point. That wasn't the important fact. What mattered was that he needed a friend and that was all that counted.

She'd heard about Hanson blowing his top, and

106

then how Don felt about the whole thing.

The bass man had said simply the night before: "He doesn't want help. Let him sink!"

And that was all the man would say about Billy Carter.

She got up and dressed. Had breakfast and then walked down to the lobby of her hotel, ordered a taxi and then went to the place where she had left Bill. She walked up to the clerk and said: "Is Bill Carter in?"

The man looked questioningly at her and then thumbed through the register, then he returned his eyes to Terry's. "He's not at the hotel anymore."

"What do you mean?" she gasped, feeling her insides go cold.

"He checked out last night."

For a moment she felt the world spinning and a blackness cloud over her vision.

"You okay, lady?" the clerk asked.

She refocused her eyes on the man's face and managed to whisper out, knowing what the answer would be, "Did he say where he was going?"

The man just smiled at her and said: "Lady, we don't ask where people come from or where they go. They come, order a room, pay their bills and then leave. That's the beginning and the end of it all!"

She turned and walked slowly from the lobby, feeling weak, confused and helpless.

It had been a mistake to leave Bill alone. She should have stayed with him.

One thing she knew, she'd have to look for him, find him, and then try to do what she could to bring him up from the gutter slime of his own bitter pain.

BLUES FOR A DEAD LOVER, BY CHARLES NUETZEL

Maybe Don would help?

Chapter Ten

Don just stared blankly at Terry.

"We have to find him!" she pleaded, frantically.

"Oh, come, Terry, don't be a little fool! He doesn't want help!" Don snapped, bitterly. "We've done everything we can. All Bill's done is get Hanson mad at him and disgusted me. If he wants to blow his life down the river 'cause of some broad that's his business. There's no reason to let him pull us down with him!"

"Well, I'm going to do what I can!"

Don stood there in the middle of his room and stared at her in amazement.

Then he said: "Don't!"

"Why not? I love him and he needs a friend!"

"He doesn't give a goddamned about you! Or anybody. He'll just use your body and when he's through, throw you aside!"

"I'm sorry, Don, there just isn't anything else I can do about it. I'm going to find him with or without your help!" she announced, turning and moving for the door.

"Just tell Hanson I'm quitting." She opened the door and then stepped out into the hall, amazed by her own determination.

This had been a good break for her, working at the club, and now she'd let it come to an end because of a man who was out in the deep end because of another woman. She shrugged to herself and sighed, walking down the hall toward her room. The first thing was to call all the hotels in town and see if they had any listings for a Bill Carter. From then on it was a matter of going to him. If it was necessary to give her body again she'd do that. What ever he wanted at first and then she'd be there when he finally got tired of running. At that point he'd be glad to have a helping hand and a friend, maybe a lover, maybe somebody he could care about at some future time. Maybe miracles happened if one simply worked hard to make them come into being.

It was several hours later before she found a hotel, on the end of town, that had a Bill Carter listed.

"Blond, good-looking?"

"That's the man. He's not in right now," the voice said over the receiver. "Want to leave a message?"

She thought that over and then finally decided it would be better not to leave one. She'd go to the hotel and then talk the clerk into letting her into the room, saying she was his wife, or lover or anything to get into the room. Then she'd wait for him.

She changed, after showering, into a light, tight fitting dress. Made her face up and then packed her clothing. She checked out of the room and then head for the *Benton Street Hotel.*

An hour later she was standing in the small, dingy lobby, looking at the night clerk.

"But he'll be expecting me!" she objected, frantically.

110

"I can't let you—"

The man stopped speaking when she presented a ten dollar bill from her purse and handed it over to him. He took it in greedy hands and then smiled crookedly. He told her the number of Bill's room..

After the man handed her a key she took up her bag and then started for the room,

It was up four flights of stairs, and by the time she got in front of the door marked 4E she was exhausted, her arm aching from the weight of the bag. Sighing heavily, she fitted the key into the door and opened it.

A moment later she was standing in the tiny room, the light on, examining the dirt and filth.

There were several bottles scattered on the floor and the dresser. The ones on the dresser were mostly filled. The room was ratty, with walls that had been marked with the fingers, what looked like spilled drinks and the clawing marks of time. The managers hadn't tried to keep the place clean. It was the kind of room a person went to when they didn't care about anything except booze and sex.

She sighed, and then started arranging things in a more orderly fashion. An hour later she settled down on the bed, a glass of raw whiskey in her hands. She would need the booze to help to keep her there.

Just then there was the sound of a key turning in the lock and then Bill Carter walked in, and following him was a cheap-looking bleached blonde, whose age and life had already marred her no doubt once pretty features.

* * * * * * *

111

Bill looked numbly at Terry, sitting on the edge of his bed. For a moment he couldn't figure out how she had gotten there or why. Then slowly through the dull fog of the liquor his mind figured out how most of it was possible. Discover where he was, bribe the clerk, come up and....

But what was she doing there?

"What you want!" he demanded, pulling the blonde pick up forward into the room.

"Say what kind of setup is this?" the blonde demanded, staggering across the room and stopping in front of Terry. She peered down at the other woman.

"You goin' for a three way?" The woman grinned crudely. "Do you want us to do it first? I mean...her and me?"

Terry just looked up coldly.

"I don't think he'll be wanting *your*...services, now!" she said, standing and moving around the woman. She stepped over to Bill and took hold of his arm.

"How are you, honey?" she asked in a coy, possessive tone of voice.

"How you get in?" Bill demanded, angrily.

"Oh that's not so hard. I've been waiting for you, Billy-boy!"

"Well!" exploded the bleach blonde, stomping toward the door.

"Hey, don't leave!" Bill cried after her.

"What kind of lady do you take me for?" the woman shouted, "I see you two have something serious going!" She opened the door, stepping angrily out and slamming it after her.

Bill didn't say anything for a long while, and

Terry moved away, smiling. Finally he stepped to the dresser where the bottles of whiskey were. Pouring himself a drink he slowly downed it. Then turned toward Terry. "Okay, what is it this time? What kind of lecture?"

"Honey, don't be silly. I came to you! That should be enough!" she told him evenly.

"What for?" he asked bitterly, pouring another shot of whiskey and looking at Terry's voluptuous figure.

She laughed, nervously and then sighed. "What do you think?" she asked, starting to move over to him. She came to a stop only a few inches from him. "I thought that you might need a friend."

"Why'd you run out, before, friend, dear friend?"

"Let's forget all about that!" she told him. "How about a drink?"

"Hell, help yourself!" he snapped, stepping away and moving to the bed. He sat down, looking at the floor.

* * * * * * *

He didn't like the setup. Terry had some reason for coming to him, and he didn't think he would be liking that, either.

It had taken all day to take the bitterness out of his mind about the blow up with Hanson. He'd moved into this place after getting some money from the bank. Then came the drinking. Later he'd gone out to a bar and started a conversation with the cheap little blonde he'd brought up to his room for a little party. Now: Terry!

113

"Say, don't you want a friend?" she asked, stepping in front of him.

"No friends! Nothing!" he snapped, gulping the whiskey and then moving to the dresser so that he could pour himself some more booze.

"How long are you going to play this sad song?" she asked carefully.

Angrily he turned, glaring at Terry. "None of your damned business!"

"Oh, okay, honey, just wondering!" she backed down.

He turned back to the dresser and looked drunkenly at the bottle of whiskey, then downed the liquor in his glass. The world slid slightly and he felt himself weaving. With a quick action he gripped hold of the dresser for balance.

Behind him he heard the rustle of a dress. Then movement.

"What is it you want?" he demanded, not turning to look at Terry.

"Does it matter?" she asked. "I'm here for you. That should be enough…for now."

He tried to think if it did matter and he couldn't come up with an answer, because nothing mattered anymore. Nothing at all.

His mind wasn't working right, that much he knew. It was dizzy from the booze he'd been downing like water the last few days; but that's the way he wanted it. Complete blackout because he didn't have the courage to kill himself the quick way. Don had been right about that. At least!

Slowly he turned around and looked at Terry.

She was standing there, staring at him, and smiling slightly, her clothes in a pile on the floor.

114

For some reason it didn't surprise him that she was completely nude. He couldn't have really cared.

One woman or the other. They all want the same thing, so what difference does it make, brother?

Give them all a fling!

Bill moved to her, folding Terry into his arms.

A moment later they were on the bed, hungrily devouring each other until sensual union had joined them into the savage lover's rhythm.

* * * * * * *

All through the evening Don Jenson had that hard bitterness choking through him at the idea of Terry Anson throwing her career out for Bill Carter. Not that he would interfere with such an arrangement between two people who were in love. But this was different. Bill didn't love Terry, and she was just making a fool of herself. There wasn't anything she could really do for the man, and Don had finally come to terms with his feeling for her.

He was falling in love with Terry.

Yet that was beside the point. He realized there wasn't a chance for him with Terry, but he didn't want to see her throwing away everything she had been trying to build. And the thought surprised him because he hadn't realized that he could be so selfless.

When the last set had been finished he had made up his mind.

He'd find out where Bill was shacked up and then get Terry away from the man. By force, if necessary. He couldn't let her waste her life on Bill at this time!

Later, maybe, but after Bill had found himself and knew exactly what he was doing, things would be different.

Don left at 2:30 in the morning to find Bill and Terry!

It wasn't until eight that morning that Don got a line as to where Bill had holed up. And then twenty minutes later he was at the hotel, questioning the clerk.

"I'm afraid you just missed them, sir," the man said in an impersonal tone of voice.

"What you talking about, man?" Don demanded.

"They checked out just ten minutes ago!"

"What?" he cried in alarm.

"That's what I said!"

"Where'd they go?"

"Look, mister, I don't question people. They checked out, paid the bill and left. That's all I know,"

Don turned and walked out, dazed and hopelessly lost. They could be anyplace. Anywhere. He'd have to check the hotels that evening, in town.

But he had the idea that they had left town. Why, he couldn't imagine. Where they might go it was anybody's guess.

He would try, but he knew that it was hopeless.

Now Bill had Terry's life under his thumb, and in his condition he would be able to destroy her.

116

Chapter Eleven

Las Vegas!

City of the hungry men and women seeking easy money and leaving hard earned cash. It had taken Bill and Terry a little over a week to drive to the desert Syndicate City, and he had allowed her to do most of the driving so that he could keep himself in a numb state of drunk. They had stopped off at motels late in the evenings and then left late in the afternoon, after their bodies had been exploited and he felt he could stand the long haul of driving.

Then the Las Vegas stop-off. Into the Sands.

Plenty of booze, eye-openers and night caps all topped off with a lot of sex.

And then down to the casino.

He was slightly drunk, just managing to keep himself on a level from the free drinks that the club kept offering him.

Everything was a blur, half fantasy, half real.

"Place it on 22," he told the roulette dealer. Then he lay back and waited for the little ball to either drop on his number or one of the other 37 possible stop-offs. If it settled in the 22 spot he'd be some thirty dollars ahead.

Vaguely he wondered where Terry was. They'd

been in Vegas for about two days now and the money had kept at an even level. But he hadn't seen Terry for at least ten hours. That was Vegas for you. Friends before you get there, and then almost strangers after that, hardly seeing each other once you've arrived.

Husbands began to hate wives and wives hate husbands. Money became a wall between two people.

He sighed as 25 turned out to be the winning number.

Then he took a drag on his cigarette and a sip from the highball.

"22 again!" he told the dealer, tossing a chip toward the man.

He thought about the nights with Terry. They had been good nights. She had the kind of body that knew how to make a man enjoy it. Make him good and hot and hungry to simply smother into her yielding, embracing flesh. Right then he could use that body, but he wasn't sure that he knew where he could find her. She might be up in the rooms, but he doubted it. She liked to gamble. Maybe she'd gone to some other club. He didn't know.

"Bill! Bill Carter!" a light, feminine voice called at his ear.

He turned to look. A tall blonde was standing there looking at him in amazement. He knew the face and figure, but couldn't place the name that must go with it. They'd had a wild weekend together some years back. That's all that he could remember about her.

"What you doing here in Vegas?" she asked, taking the seat next to him.

"Same as everybody else."

The woman laughed, bending slightly over and peering deep into his eyes.

"Not every *body* else!" she breathed in a low whisper.

Suddenly he remembered a lot about what had happened before. She was Sara Cummings, and she'd had quite a crush on him two years back.

The dress that she was wearing was low-cut and tight fitting. It was designed to offer a good look at her natural treasures. Golden in color.

"What you doing here?" he asked, hardly really interested.

"In one of the shows. Chorus thing." She smiled, and reached out a hand to touch his fingers. He ignored the contact.

She had the body for that kind of work. A show girl deluxe.

They didn't say anything for a while and then finally she said: "How long are you staying?"

"Don't know!"

She looked down and then suddenly moved her eyes back toward his.

"Why don't you come up to the room so we can talk over old times?" she suggested.

"Who wants to talk?" he groused.

"Who does?" she agreed. "Not me. Not verbally, anyway."

That was Sara. Her pants were always so hot that she needed a man in them almost all the time. The thought of giving it to her abruptly appealed to him.

"Number 22!" the dealer called.

A moment later he was given a stack of chips.

"Cash them!" he told the man.

After the stack of silver dollars had been handed over Bill turned toward the woman.

He remembered how much fun she could be.

"I'm not interested in conversation," he told her, bluntly, letting his eyes feast over her lovely body.

"Well, come with me, then!" she invited, taking his hand warmly in hers. "We can let our bods do the talking, if you get what I mean."

Why not, he thought, *take her up on the deal!* He wanted more booze and he was more than interested in being with a woman, and Terry wasn't around. And what she didn't know wouldn't hurt her. And anyway it wasn't any of her business. He hadn't asked her to come with him; she knew the score.

"Okay let's go up and talk!" he told Sara, standing and taking her arm. "Want a drink, first?"

"No! I have some bottles up in the room. We can booze it up there, while we...talk!" she told him, her eyes flashing excitedly. "Gee, it's good to see you again. Been over two years. And what luck! I'd just run out of...friends!" she chattered. "What do you think of that? A girl with my shape running out of friends!"

"Everybody has their dry times!" he commented evenly. He could pretty well guess what had happened. She'd knocked it with most of the men she knew and they were shying away from her. Sara's need for a man could burn a guy up in a very short time. A sex night with her wasn't just a couple of quickies. It continued with every possible variation that she could think up. The kind that Bill could really use, right then. She wanted endless sex. In fact she'd told him about one time being with a

120

couple of men at once and proudly announced how she'd knocked them totally out of commission after a night of it.

"You been exhausting your lovers again?" he laughed, patting her fanny in a rather brazen way. She didn't even mind that being done in public.

"I suppose so. You never wore out with me, though," she stated, voice suddenly low and husky. "You almost bombed me out!"

He laughed at that. "Flattery will get you…"

"Laid, I hope!" she whispered. "I have so much to talk to you about. We could talk all night and day and through a few more nights and days! Well…okay, I'll give you the short versions of my life and times."

"I hope not too short," he chuckled, actually enjoying her. Maybe that's just want he needed, some woman that didn't mean a thing, whom he would never need to worry about seeing again—she was out for kicks without strings of any kinds.

"I would say not!" she promised. "I'll last as long as you wanna…continue the conversation! You remember how I am. Needy greedy. Never enough to wear me out!"

She was a fun lady in bed, that much he knew. Nice, but for a nympho Sara considered herself respectable. She wouldn't take up with a pickup. She had to know the man first. Introduced formally. Of course it wasn't difficult to fix up an introduction; and once that happened, she'd pull her pants off first chance she got.

They walked arm in arm down to her room and she took out her key and opened the door. They stepped in and she closed the door after them.

"Well, what do you think, Bill?"

"About what?" he asked.

"Sex first? Or drink first?" she said, coming out boldly and setting the mood for what was going to take place without any game-playing.

He looked at her tall trim figure and idly considered stripping it right then and there. But he decided the drink first was in order. And then there was a rather pleasant thought that occurred to him. It came in the form of a memory. Once they'd taken a bath together, and the idea suddenly appealed to him.

"Drink first. With a shower afterwards!" he ordered.

She squealed excitedly. "Why I didn't think you'd remember about that! How thrilling!" she cried, moving to the dresser where there were a couple of bottles. "Want whiskey, rum, scotch?"

"Scotch! If it's all the same with you!" he told her, stepping to the bed and sitting down on the edge of it. She was sitting beside him in a few moments.

"What you been doing since I saw you last?" she asked, taking hold of his hand and placing it on her leg.

"Blowing some hot gigs for a while…. But that's over," he said bitterly.

"Over?" she cried in surprise, pressing his fingers into the softness of her flesh.

"Long story I don't want to talk about!" he said firmly, letting his fingers take in the soft warmness of her.

"Okay. What you want to talk about? Sex?"

He didn't answer that.

"You in town alone?" she inquired, giving him a

sidelong glance.

"No!"

"Oh!" Her voice was disappointed sounding. "Wife or girl?"

"Girl!"

"Wouldn't she be mad you being up here in a room with another woman?" she asked.

"Who cares!" he choked out in a husky voice. The nearness of Sara was beginning to affect him. She had an eagerness about sex that worked a man to a fever pitch very quick!

He gulped on the scotch and noticed her reaction.

"You really belt them. I never knew you drank heavily!" she observed, sliding closer and running a finger tip along his leg.

"I belt them!" he replied, tiredly.

"And I *un*-belt them," she laughed, hand reaching down to his belt. "Should I do the honors? Zip, zip?"

He shrugged. "Whatever turns you on."

"You do. All of you!"

"That's what you say to all your lovers."

"So…I love 'em all. All over. You remember!"

"Sure. The hot Cummings girl."

"You make that sound so…gosh all mighty hot and sexy."

"Just like you," he countered on automatic.

He vaguely wondered why he was here. What he was doing in her room. It had happened so fast, without any build up that suddenly it seemed all out of place. One moment he'd been sitting at the roulette table and then she was sitting next to him. One quick offer to come here with her and then the next second he was starting sex party.

Suddenly she crushed her mouth onto his, her tongue not waiting for him to respond. He felt its moistness probe past his lips and then he parted his teeth so that it could dig deeper.

The taste of her was pleasant and exciting. Her arms slid around his neck as she drew herself to him. For a long time they kissed, exploring each other's mouths and then finally she came up for air. "Okay, strip! And let's get into the shower. I'm burning!"

"You always are."

"Oh, but I mean it real bad. You got me so hot!"

He laughed at that. "Sure, all my fault!"

She stood and started removing her dress. It came off swiftly. Then she reached around and un-clasped her bra and it flung off her breasts, giving them freedom. They weren't as large as Terry's and fell a little lower. But they were exciting, just standing there, the nipples tilted slightly up, already firmly erect. She leaned close, giggling, her breasts swaying inches from his lips.

"Why don't you kiss them hello?" she asked, throatily. "They just hurt so hard for you're soft, wet kisses."

He laughed and stood.

"Let's play it slow and easy. Enjoy it." He paused and then said: "I want another drink."

"Help yourself!" she offered, slipping her finger tips under the elastic of her pink panties. Slowly she drew them down from around wide hips, so that he was able to see she was a natural blonde.

"Honey, you can't imagine how I want you in that shower." Her voice was a rasp.

124

He felt his pulse speed at the sight of her. He gulped down the hard passion knot in his throat and then stepped to the dresser, poured himself a drink and downed it in one gulp. The whiskey burned down his throat and into his stomach. A moment later it heated through each nerve and cell of his body.

He felt slender, delicate hands. slide around his waist and then quick moving fingers unclasp his pants.

"Give it to me now! Before!" she cried in a voice tight with agony. "I want my cocktail, right now."

He spun around and faced Sara. Her eyes were closed and her lips open and moist. Without a thought he reached.

She squirmed convulsively to him, and then before he knew what was happening she had pulled him around so that her back was to the wall and then thrust against him, moans and cries breaking from her tormented and trembling lips.

Her hands clawed at his back and her body was convulsively thrashing against his, screaming to be taken instantly, without waiting a moment longer.

It didn't take long to steam him up over the point of control and then the exhaustion of release left the two of them clinging to each other, breathing heavily, sweat beginning to oil the surface of their skin.

Finally she moved slightly in his arms and then whispered in his ear: "I think we can use that bath, now!" she paused and then slid out away from him, taking his hand and pulling it. A moment later they were stepping into the small shower.

"Hurry! Let's have some fun!" Sara fairly screamed, clawing at his arm.

He turned and looked at her, his eyes steaming with hunger again. That was the way Sara effected men.

"Oh...God!" she sighed, her eyes closing, as a convulsive shudder rushed through her body.

Her lips thrust forward, ramming into his and working hard and violently there.

He let his hands caress her breasts until her actions were whipping her so passionately against him that he couldn't stand it any longer.

He felt her claw at him, pulling him to her with trembling hands and fairly screaming in her pleasure filled agony.

"Its so hard! Oh, do it hard!" she cursed at him, grabbing at him. "I want that right in here!"

Her fingers instantly gripped hungrily at him, directing, pushing, pulling. "Yes. There...oh, honey, deep in me!"

She worked her body savagely to his.

"Hard and brutal! The way I like it!" she cried, squirming her breasts against his chest.

The moisture of the shower caused her body to cling to his; the skin sliding heatedly on his skin.

She moaned and thrashed and jerked. Then suddenly the peak thrust them brutally against one another and he felt every muscle in her strain against the ecstasy and pleasure she was experiencing around him.

Finally she relaxed and then laughed excitedly. "You're good! So good! Just like I remembered. Here, let me clean you. Let me caress you with soap. Let's see if you can do me again!" She suited the action to her words, taking a small hotel bar of soap and working it on his body. Rubbing his chest and arms with a delighted giggle. Finally down to his waist and then his legs. She saved the best part for last and then finally handed him a bar of soap and urged his fingers into the swells of her breasts.

"Do it good! Make it exciting! Make me want another of your special cocktails!" she sighed, tightening against him before letting him begin cleaning her.

She moaned and squirmed all the time, from the moment he soaped her breasts until the nipples were hidden, until he finished with her stomach and legs.

"Oh, God you're good! You really know!" she said clawing at him. "I want it again. Now! Don't wait! Not a minute longer!" she rasped in his ear, biting it with her lips.

"I can't go all night!" he commented.

But she squirmed against him, violently, working her body against his until she was crying in agony.

"God!" she sobbed in pleasure. She urged him along her body. Clawing his hands deep into the fiery, burning flesh that trembled convulsively under his touch, while all the time trying to build the peak in his body.

Finally he felt himself being overwhelmed again, beyond a point where he never thought he could be pushed. Her demanding force could build a fire under an iceberg, and he was far from that.

She begged him to take her once more in the shower, and the way her hands moved over him he couldn't control the urge any longer, he couldn't hold back.

They surged together, their breaths heavy and heaving in their chest. Then the thrusting and jerking and straining finally left them weak and exhausted; even leaving her momentarily satisfied.

They stepped from the shower and then dried each other.

"I need a drink!" she told him, rushing into the other room, toward the dresser. A moment later she moved to the bed with two glasses filled with scotch. She quickly pulled aside the covers and slid under.

"Come on! What you waiting for?" she asked, laughingly in total delight, her eyes feasting on his groin. "I want a lot more of that! I just love drinkin' your cocktails!"

He slid in next to her, moving as close as he could so that their hips and legs were touching. Then he felt her leg move over his. She smiled at him and then took a drink from the glass in her hand.

"You dick a girl real good!" she told him, taking hold of his hand and moving it under the blankets and down to the smooth flatness of her stomach. The skin quivered under his fingers. "You're the best I've ever had for a long time, you know!"

"Oh, come on!" he cried, gulping from the glass of scotch.

"No! That's the truth. That's why I was so glad to see you downstairs. You know there's been plenty of men…that was only a story I told you. The minute I saw you I wanted you right away. And I was determined to have you! Right in here!"

She put his hand between her legs and squeezed around it. "Right in here."

128

He just nodded his head and smiled.

"You make it burn nice, Bill. I always enjoyed our times together. You're super. A big super dupe of a stud!"

He'd never thought of himself as being so great as a lover; but she should know. If there was ever any expert, it would be Sara and her overcharged body that demanded and demanded beyond the ability of any man to fully satisfy.

"What you doing with your hand?" she asked, raising her eyebrows.

"Nothing!"

"That's just it!" she complained frowning. "Why'd you think I put it there?"

He laughed and then went about giving her the pleasure she was begging for, his finger caressing her, deeply.

"Yes, oh, that's nice. Right into my temple of love. Just walk 'em in and search for the treasures."

She tensed against him, her thighs parted and then she leaned back. "Find the jewels. And make them sizzle!"

One thought moved through his mind as their bodies blended together thirty minutes later: She was the best—if he lost Terry she'd fill in very nicely.

That thought faded as her greedy body gulped tightly about him, churning furiously in its raw, savage, unlimited hunger.

He heard her sobbing and even screaming in pleasure, but it was a distant sound, for his own sensations had been totally smothered in the wildness of her total possession of him. The lights faded and then burst into a blaze of ecstasy.

Chapter Twelve

Terry had been standing at the dollar slot machine for over three hours. It was like a sickness with her, each dollar being just another possible chance at the $600 jackpot. Or more. Each dollar only one more unit toward a small pot that would help to keep them going. But it was something else for her. An escape from what she had become and what Bill Carter was making her into. Many men thought of a woman like her as a tramp. She had never considered that to be true. Now for the first time she was beginning to wonder.

All her life she'd had hot pants for one man or another, even allowing herself to be picked up by some slob in a bar when she was loaded. But this was something different. There had always been some logical rationalization that she could fall back on. Drunk. Her need for sex. But with Bill it had turned into something completely different. She'd let her singing drop to a gutter. And what was far worst was the fact that she'd flushed her body down to the gutter level. And not for love. There had been times in the past when she'd given herself to a man she was in love with. But this was different in that the man didn't love her in the least. He used her.

130

And she was letting him do that!

She dropped another dollar into the slot and pulled down the handle.

Cherry.

Lemon.

Bar.

Two dollars dropped into the slot.

"Would you let the management buy you a drink?" a light feminine voice asked her.

"Whiskey Sour," she ordered, placing another dollar in the slot and pulling the handle.

She wondered where it was all going to end.

Lemon.

Cherry.

Orange.

Would it be a lemon? She didn't know. Bill and her. Bill was drinking his life down the drain and she realized that she was letting him pull her down with him.

Bitterly she dropped another dollar and pulled the handle once more.

Maybe it had been a mistake? She didn't know. All she knew was that she'd had to be away from Bill for a few hours, and that was why she'd come into downtown Vegas, away from the strip with all its clown like glamour.

Ever since Bill had gotten the harebrained idea to drive west to Las Vegas, Terry had had that terrible feeling that her life, as it had been in the past, was over.

Cherry. Cherry. Lemon.

Five dollars clanked down.

Terry sighed and dropped one more silver dollar, not really caring what happened.

Three oranges dropped into place and ten dollars rattled in the little bucket at the bottom of the machine.

Bill was a good lover. And if he ever snapped out of his running and escaping he could be a good human being again. Maybe go to the trumpet again.

She sighed.

Bar.

Bar.

Orange.

A slight excitement had cramped through Terry as she had seen the two bars fall into place. The thrill of almost, but not quite, making the jackpot of $600 had stabbed the need and necessity to try some more. If she could play the machine long enough she it was sure to hit. That was the temptation which drove her to just one more try.

Another five dollars dropped in, but nothing returned. For five minutes more she kept dropping dollars as fast as she could, getting nothing in return.

One more and she would quit, she thought.

Nothing!

She started stepping away and then remembered the free drink she'd ordered. She had to wait for that, at least.

Terry sighed tiredly and put another dollar into the machine, pulling the handle down once more.

One bar and two oranges wrong order to pay off.

She sighed heavily and put in another dollar.

"Terry Anson! Is that really you?"

She turned, startled at hearing her name.

There was a tall man standing behind her, grinning in delight.

"You're sure a sight!" he cried.

"Dave!" Terry yelled in excitement. "What you doing here in town?"

"Blowing a gig here at the casino," the man said, putting a friendly hand on her shoulder.

"Still blowing the sax "

"Well more than that! Have a small combo of my own!" he told her. For a long time they just stood there gazing at each other. She'd known Dave Baxter off and on for ten years or more. Several times she'd worked with him; nothing more. He was a loyal married man with six kids.

Terry heard the clank of money in the little slot machine bucket and looked at the three plums that had registered on the machine. That made $14 for her. She gathered up the money just a young woman stepped up to her and handed a "free" drink from the management, which she downed quickly.

"Let's go some place to talk," she said, suddenly getting an idea. "I want to ask you a favor."

Dave Baxter's eyes rose. "See you for two seconds and you're the scheming woman ranting for favors!" he laughed. "I'm still a married man."

"I know."

"And no matter how much you flirt you won't get me into your tangled passionate web. Darn. But I'm one of those square headed freaks."

"I know. Loyal to the end. And what an end you have!" She laughed, brazenly patted his fanny. "Nice and hard-assed."

"Keep that up and you'll cause me real problems."

"I could take care of that."

"Oh how I know. I've heard what you can do to a man!"

They were walking arm in arm through the noisy casino.

"Do I have that terrible a reputation?" she asked, suddenly uncomfortable.

"Not at all."

"That's a lie, isn't it?"

"Well, word does get around that you're something very special."

"Oh, Dave, you sure have a lovely line. What a shame you're all locked up and untouchable."

"Sometimes, like now, I wish it were different, but, alas, I'm an—"

"Ass!" she giggled.

"What?"

"Well it rhymes. Alas and ass!"

He laughed at that. "Come think of it, you're probably right."

"Where can we go to talk in private?" she asked, putting the silver dollars in her purse. It became heavy with its new load.

"My hotel room if you're not afraid of a married man!" he suggested, lightly.

"Of you? Hell, Dave, you won't look at a woman who had her clothes stripped off. In fact it is said you'd cover a naked girl up with your cloak of honor!"

"Well, that's sometimes tarnished—but you're probably right!"

"Dare I tempt you?"

He laughed nervously. "Don't try it, Terry. I wouldn't want to be tempted..."

It was the same old chatter that the two of them

134

had enjoyed so many times in the past. He was a good sport and a nice guy. She just hoped that he'd be more than just that. She hoped he might be a solution.

"How are the kids? And wife?" she asked conversationally as they stepped out onto the street and headed south for the Fremont Hotel.

"Fine. Fine. They're coming up in a few days on a vacation." He paused and looked at her, saying: "You planning on being in town long?"

"Don't know," she sighed. "It could be for a few more days or a few more weeks or maybe months. I'll tell you when we are at your place."

They didn't say much after that until they were in his room. Then he offered her a drink. "Don't have much, but...what I have is for my friends."

"Anything will do," she said, sinking into a chair and half closing her eyes. She was tired. Tired in the way that only Las Vegas could make a person tired. The town was an insanity that got into your blood the moment you stepped into it, charging the nerves and pushing the body beyond the normal point of energy, until you were so dragged out that you could hardly think. Night and day blended and had no meaning at all. Just the machines and tables and continual noise.

Just one more dollar into the machine!

Just another hand of blackjack.

Just one more time.

Maybe this time you'd win.

Just one more time.

Another roll of the dice to make your point!

Just one more time.

A drink, a man, some sex.

Just one more time.

"Here you are, Terry," Dave's voice interrupted her thoughts. He handed her a glass half filled with whiskey. "No mixer, sorry."

"That's all right. You know me. Anything with booze in it!"

He sat on the bed, facing her, leaning his elbows on his legs. "Well, shoot!"

She started to tell him. First slowly and then finally warming up to the story about Bill. She told him all that she knew. He listened in silence and when she was finished just sat looking at her for a long time before saying anything. Finally he sighed and then asked: "Why, tell me?"

"Well you know Bill Carter."

"Of course. Who doesn't in the music world? The tops." Then he sighed, deeply. "A damned shame blowing his career over a dead chick. Funny thing...I never thought he'd fall. But they say the ones that fight the hardest fall the hardest. He was one of the fastest men in the business with the women."

"Can you help him?" Terry asked, nervously finishing her drink.

"How?"

"If I brought him up to the club when you were on stage and you just happened to see him, couldn't you call him up to blow a set? I think that maybe if he got that trumpet to his lips one time he'd maybe regain his interest."

Dave looked doubtful.

"Not likely. But...I'll do anything I can for a fellow music man," he said, smiling. "And for a pretty girl."

136

"Thanks!" Terry stood, to leave. "Just tell me when you go on and I'll see what I can do to get him here about that time. You haven't seen me. It'll all be a drop in surprise. If he thought I'd set it up he'd blow his top!"

Dave nodded, knowingly and then extended his hand to Terry's. "On from twelve on with breaks every twenty minutes for twenty minutes. Another group comes on as we go off, then we take over as they go off. The circle thing…you know one musician at a time changing places so that there's continued music without a break. The change over is swift from one group to the next in that manner."

Twenty minutes later Terry was back in her hotel room in the Sands, wondering what had happened to Bill. She'd looked around the whole hotel, but he wasn't to be found. He'd disappeared. But that wasn't really so unusual, since it was easy to drop out of sight in Las Vegas. Run to another hotel with the hope that your luck will change at a different location. Fat chance.

Terry undressed and then fell exhausted, nude across the bed.

In less than three minutes she was sound asleep.

* * * * * * *

Bill slowly turned the key in the lock and opened the door. A moment later he was inside his room, turned on the light and moved toward the bed. He was exhausted and still slightly loaded. In the past few days he'd been tapering off a little; not because he wanted to, so much, but rather because booze was beginning to have a bad effect on his stomach. He could only keep down enough to get him high, but not plastered the way he wanted to be.

And there was another thing that was changing in him. It was summed up in the form of a question: *How long could he continue being drunk?*

But he had managed to ignore the answer, because he didn't like the panic it caused to move through him.

Terry was lying on her stomach on the bed, crossways.

He looked at the rounded two bulges of her fanny and vaguely felt an urge to place his hands on them. But the thought reminded him of Sara Cummings and her demanding, ever demanding body he had just left and had completely drained him of all possible chance of completing anything that he might start with Terry. Sure there were other ways to satisfy a woman, but he wasn't in the mood for anything except sleep.

He was in one word: exhausted.

"Terry!" he said in a rasp, taking hold of her arm and half lifting and half dragging her body to one side of the bed.

Her eyes opened and she looked up at him.

"Hey, where have you been?" she asked, squinting slightly.

"Around!" he told her, avoiding the necessity of lying to her directly. He hadn't decided exactly what he was going to do about her and Sara. If anything.

He wanted them both. Or rather he felt that he owed Terry more than just a quick brush off. She'd been taking a lot of crap from him the last days. When he said to jump she jumped. When he told her to pull off her pants that's what she had done. No matter how little he cared about himself and his life since Laura was no more, he couldn't bring himself to kick Terry right into the teeth. She was an amazingly nice person.

On the other hand, he felt a strong urge to have Sara. No strings attached Sara. Ideal for a man in his situation; for a man who didn't want any emotional lines touching him. This was a woman who could never feel love for a man, because her body demanded more than any one man could give her. It was one ball after another with Sara. And he wanted that kind of an arrangement. With Terry he couldn't help having the sense of guilt, because he knew she was trying to play the game to win him. She was in love and he was taking advantage of it. And, strangely, he felt guilty about that. Laura had warned him.

"What you thinking?" Terry asked, as he slid down next to her.

"Nothing!"

"You look concerned, worried!"

"Oh, shut up!" he snapped, trying to keep his head from throbbing too hard.

"You hung over?" she asked, almost tenderly.

"What you think?" he countered, bitterly. His words seemed to have no effect on her. She never seemed to show anger. That was annoying. He couldn't make her mad. She was always there with understanding. Quiet and waiting for him; not hearing the insults he threw her way; not aware of the contempt of his voice when he spoke to her. She waited. And he knew what for: him to change.

For him to "snap" out of it; the only thing was that he didn't plan on snapping out of it ever!

"Anything I can do?" Her hand touched his shoulder.

"Yes! Leave me alone! I need some sleep!"

Her hand withdrew and he felt her turn away from him. He vaguely wondered how long she could take his crap without exploding. He wished she would blow her top. He wished he could get rid of her without hurting her. But he realized that it would be impossible. She had sold herself. Her respect. Everything she had sold out on the slim chance that when he "snapped" out of it, he would want her.

Sighing he closed his eyes and tried to blot out all awareness. He needed sleep; needed complete black out.

He lay there for a long while, not able to find restful sleep. Finally he turned and put his arm around Terry.

A shock jolted through him.

One realization had caused it: Terry felt so good!

"Terry," he whispered, pulling her around and sliding closer.

"Yes?" she said sleepily, not opening her eyes. He relaxed and then moved away from her, lying on his back and looking up at the ceiling.

How long would it take before the bitter edge of the hurt deep down inside him to finally numbed at least slightly. He wondered if it would ever dull. The terrible knowledge of knowing that he would never have Laura again ate away at his very center and made him want to run and hide in some black well, pulling the top over him. Never to hold her in his arms was a bitter reality impossible to face.

A choke tightened in his throat and he closed his eyes against the tears welling there. He needed dear Laura but she wasn't anywhere but in her grave, dead and lost to him forever.

He sighed and tried to relax. Consciously he thought about each muscle relaxing. Soothed each nerve with a powerful surge of will power. It was a kind of meditation trick he'd learned years before. The woman who had taught him gave it some voodoo eastern religious name. Hocus Pocus. Mantra and all. He accepted it for what it was: self-hypnosis.

Finally rest slowly started to ebb around his mind and then began clouding into blackness.

He heard Laura's voice call to him: "Bill, oh, Bill, where are you?"

"Here! Here!" he cried in a desperate voice, looking around him. Finally he spotted her on the bed beside him, her body draped in a frilly blue negligee.

She smiled and reached her arms out to Bill. "I've been waiting for a long time. So very long for you to come to me. What kept you?"

He started to say that it was because she was dead, but she seemed to have guessed his thought and quickly hushed him with the palm of her hand pressing against his lips.

"Don't say it. Just come into my arms and make love. Fill me with love. Caress my flesh until it is fiery with desire. Run your hands along my body until I can't stand it any longer. Then gently take me. Be so gentle!" She was sobbing in his ear and then suddenly the scene changed and they were sitting in an airplane, clutching each other desperately. He

felt fear and knew that the shivering of her body against his wasn't caused by passion or desire. It was sobbing and it was raw fear.

"We're going to die. We're going to die!" she screamed, terrified.

"But together!" he told her, trying to smile bravely.

She looked up into his face and then her lips moved, smiling in return. "This is the way it was meant to happen. To die in the arms of love!"

The plane was spinning now, downwards, ever downwards, until suddenly there was a series of screams from the people around them and then a jarring crash.

"Wake up! Wake up! Bill! Bill!" Terry's voice cried, her hand shaking his shoulder.

Slowly he opened his eyes. Sweat was pouring from his body and his hands were shaking.

"Oh, God!" he sobbed, covering his face with his hands. "Oh, God!"

He felt Terry pull him into her arms and press his head against her breasts. "Relax, darling. It was only a dream. Just a dream!" she said over and over, patting his head very much like a mother might with her child.

Abruptly the terror and agony left Bill's mind, and the remaining awareness was the close pressure of Terry's breasts, just a fraction from his lips.

Desire welled, suddenly. Desire that was desperate and demanding. A demand to escape frantically into the spell of a woman's passion and body so that the terror and horror of that dream could be pressed down into a deep hole of his mind and then covered over so that he wouldn't think about it any

142

more.

Her breasts were rising and falling with her breath and he could hear the beating of her heart under his ear.

The intimate nearness of the woman's body excited him, rushing a tingling sensation through his every nerve. He moved his lips, caressing the silken, full flesh beneath them.

He heard a startled intake of breath as Terry realized what he was doing. She tensed for a moment and then relaxed. A moment later the two of them slid down, full length on the bed, moving their bodies gently together.

He wanted to take his time; making the most of it, taking care to get as much pleasure out of the act as possible. Escaping into the sensual silk of her flesh until he could think of nothing else but consuming the fire that it had whipped through him.

Her lips came first.

And as their tongues met, he felt an anxious drive moving Terry's body. It had been over a day, maybe two, since she'd had him, and he could tell by her ready responses that she was more than anxious.

He moved to her breasts, almost worshipping them until he felt her churning and moaning and shivering, pleading for him to become part of her.

But he still took his time until agonized cries burst from Terry's lips and he knew she couldn't stand it any longer. He surged down to her and they savagely and brutally whipped against each other until there was nothing left but exhaustion.

Chapter Thirteen

It was eleven in the evening when Terry suggested to Bill that they go into town and see what might be doing there.

"What for? We have everything we want here!" he told her, firmly.

"Oh, come on, it'll be a change for you!"

"I don't feel like going! That's it! The end!" he stormed back at her, standing from the bed and moving over to where a couple of bottles of scotch were sitting on the dresser. What he needed was a drink. A good and strong one.

He was still bothered about what he was going to do about Terry and himself. He knew that he'd have to dump her some time. It couldn't go on forever. And then there was Sara. He knew how to get along with her; she wouldn't tire of a man that gave her sex every time she wanted it. With her body he would be able to escape from the hell of the world, complete escape; not the kind that Terry had given him.

He gulped the scotch, thrilling as it burned down his throat and into his stomach. It took several seconds to get any affect. And then he gulped again on the bottle.

"You getting loaded again?" Terry objected from the bed.

"Oh, shut up!" he bellowed, turning savagely toward the woman.

"What's gotten into you?" Terry asked, more concern in her voice than anger. She had gotten used to his nastiness by now. She hadn't reacted.

He stared at the woman and wondered if he might not put an end to it right then. It would be the best thing for her. But something held Bill back. He couldn't bring himself to hurt her that much. Somehow, he realized, he actually cared about what she might feel—saw her as a human being with deep feelings.

"I gotta get out of here for a while!" he told her gulping on the bottle one time more before putting it down and reaching for his clothes. He decided to dress and then look up Sara.

"Where you going?" she asked, desperation welling in her voice.

"Out for a while!" he snapped, opening the door.

"Can't we go into town? I wanted to be there so—"

"Then go!" he yelled, stepped into the hallway and slamming the door behind him.

Sweat was breaking out on his forehead and he couldn't quite understand what it was that had caused such a nervous reaction. Then a thought passed through his mind: *because he was taking the first steps of ditching Terry.*

He walked down the hall, in the direction of Sara's room. When he got there he knocked on the door. And waited.

145

Silence.

"Sara, are you there?" he called through a half drunken haze.

No answer.

Taking a deep breath he moved away. Maybe a little cards would settle his nerves. His whole body was edgy. But first a few drinks.

Twenty minutes later he was sitting at a black jack table with a stack of twenty dollar chips in front of him. His head was fuzzy from the liquor, but he was able to work his brain in an orderly fashion so that he knew what he was doing with the cards and what they were doing for him.

He got a five and a seven and considered taking another card. A ten would break him, but a nine would make the point He decided to try another.

He scratched the table with the two cards and the dealer placed one face up in front of him. A queen.

That broke him. Another twenty gone.

He put two chips in front of him this time.

The cards were dealt out again and he drew a nine and queen. He held and then the dealer turned up eighteen.

"Dealer pays nineteen!" he said, flipping Bill's cards over and then shoved two twenty dollar chips to him in that automatic, professional way that all the personnel of the Vegas clubs had developed over the years.

Bill vaguely wondered what he was going to do. He'd needed Sara's body to burn the taste of Terry out of his mind. She confused him; and he didn't know exactly what he felt about her.

He was caring too much about hurting or not

146

hurting the woman. And he didn't like that.

He wasn't supposed to care about anything but himself, not women, not booze.

A thought stabbed into sharp focus: *how much booze would it take to kill him.*

The idea hadn't really occurred to him consciously before, but he was fully aware of what the results of his actions would get him. *Dead! If he kept it up.* But that thought didn't frighten him. It only startled Bill to think that he hadn't actually given it much thought. But drinking oneself to death was a slow way to the grave yard.

He shrugged as the dealer took a chip away from him.

He tripled up and waited for the cards.

They came. A jack. Then an ace.

He held his breath and then waited.

"Insurance," the dealer offered, indicating the dealer's ace which was showing face up.

For a moment Bill had the urge to cover his bet, then rejected the idea.

The dealer looked under and then his eyes moved from player to player. A woman wanted to be hit. He gave her a card and then another. Then he turned up his card and announced: "Dealer pays 21."

He handed Bill forty-five dollars in chips.

Let it ride, he thought, boldly.

The next hand was a three and an eight.

A ten would make twenty-one.

"Hit me!"

A three.

Bill looked at the dealer's face card. It was a king. If he had a ten underneath there was only one way Bill could beat him. He needed a seven. On the other hand if the man didn't have a ten buried there was a chance that Bill might go broke, getting over twenty-one. There were $75 dollars on his cards.

What the hell! he decided inwardly. He'd take the chance. One more card.

It was an ace. Great help!

That gave him a total of fifteen. The only way he could win the bet was if the dealer went broke.

The woman who was hit happy took a card. It was a seven.

She held.

Dealer's card went face up. He had a ten that had been showing and a two that had been face down. He gave himself a card. It was a queen and Bill breathed a deep sigh.

There was a stack of $150 dollars in front of him.

He wondered if he should pull back the stack or let them stay there. He played a hunch.

Stayed.

The two cards were blackjack and an ace.

Bill's heart jumped and then the dealer went broke.

"I'll take that in cash," he told the dealer. "And cash in these, too."

He walked away from the table with $375 dollars profit, and had come there with only a hundred. That gave him almost five bills.

He stood watching roulette for a moment and then decided to blow the hundred that he'd come down with from the hotel room. He had nothing to lose.

He asked for a stack of $5 chips and sat down.

148

He decided on number 24, covering it from all sides at once. The corners and the lines. That took 16 chips with two on each position and then the four remaining he placed on the number itself. Quickly he did some mental adding. It would gross him something like $1,200, if he made the point.

The ball went round and round and then finally bounced into the numbers line and finally into...

"Number twenty-three!"

Bill's heart jumped. For a moment he thought that it had been the golden bell. But then he relaxed as he saw a stack of chips coming his way. He'd been on two corners and one line spot on 23.

His mind raced frantically. That cleared him around $360. He decided to play it careful, now.

He was ahead. But what he needed was a drink.

A good strong one.

"Can I get a drink?" he asked the dealer.

The man nodded and then said: "Place your bets. Place your bets" He turned and tapped a cocktail waitress on the shoulder and pointed toward Bill.

"Can the house buy you a drink?" she asked, stepping up to him.

"If you'll make it a triple shot!" he told her.

She looked startled and started to object and caught herself and turned toward the dealer. He nodded and then smiled at Bill.

"Guess so." Then she left.

In the background a jazz group started blowing. He listened for a moment until he heard that it wasn't anything exciting. Just jumping noise.

He placed a stack of five chips on number 5. Another on 6. Then one chip on 23 for a possible repeater.

"Ten!" the man called out a little while later, taking in all the chips. "No winners."

Bill tried the careful approach again.

Nothing.

He decided to take a bold chance. Roulette could get pretty dull after awhile and he wanted excitement.

Real: Excitement!

He decided to plunge.

Taking a stack of ten he covered two numbers and then the rest of the chips he put between the two, on the corner below.

1-2.

Either one would give him a winning. On 45 he'd get something back. He waited as the ball went into action, holding his breath. The little white pellet rolled into 3, bounced and then fell to number 1 and bounced again settling finally into 22.

He sighed, disappointed.

He could quit or try again.

He started to get up and then remembered the drink. He got some more chips and then settled back. In ten minutes he had managed to lose two hundred dollars, leaving himself a clear $400 more or less.

The drink came and he gulped on it a couple of times, half heartedly placing a stack of five on number six.

Number 7, five more chips.

"Repeater 36."

Bill gulped his drink and started scattering chips over the board.

He'd put out $150, covering a dozen numbers,

straight up.

"Double 0."

He had only two hundred left. Still a hundred ahead from when he'd started at the blackjack game.

He finished the drink and then relaxed momentarily, letting the liquor work through his system. A feeling of daring rushed through him. He decided to blow the whole bit on a series of three numbers, completely covering them.

Two hundred dollars worth of chips. Forty chips. Ten chips on each number and five chips on the lines between. He decided on 10-11-12. If eleven came up it should gross him something like $2,000. *And what the hell,* he thought, drunkenly, *they were either going to clean him out, or he was going to walk away with something.*

And the best thing to do was to drop your money on the line and win or lose, walk away after the ball bounces.

The little white pellet started spinning and Bill found himself sweating. It seemed as if his face was flushed. He knew his breath was coming in hard gasps.

One way he was almost hoping that he lost. He wouldn't be tempted to do any more gambling; if he won, it might keep him there.

The ball bounced.

17.

Over to 33.

Across to 6.

Slowed, stopped in 5, spun and then jumped.

"Number 10!"

Bill's heart leaped. He felt himself going dizzy with glory. $2,000 at least. The easiest money he'd ever seen in his life!

"Cash on it!" he told the man. "Cash!"

Twelve minutes later he was rushing up to the front of the door that led to the rooms he shared with Terry. He had to tell her the good news!

He flung the door open and rushed in. The room was empty.

He froze, disappointment running down his spine, icing it. Then he remembered that she had been hot to go to town. Maybe he should go in and look for her. The thought excited him; give him something to do. Even if it would be difficult, if not impossible, to find her in town.

Slowly he moved from the room and then after closing the door, down the hall. He had just stepped into the casino when a tall pretty form moved up to him.

"Well, hello, big boy!" Sara Cummings greeted him, "fancy finding you here!"

He decided not to go to town after all.

"You doing anything, special?" he asked, reaching for her arm.

"Not a thing, just did the last show, and am free as a bird until tomorrow afternoon." She smiled at him, knowingly. "You have some ideas?"

"You bet!"

"What?" she asked in a coy voice, squeezing nearer him.

"First some drink and then some place private!"

She grinned delightedly and then nodded toward the cocktail lounge, where a group was playing on the small stage. "In there?"

For answer he pulled her in that direction.

To hell with Terry! he thought drunkenly, moving toward the lounge. One girl or another?

> *One woman or the other.*
> *They all want the same thing.*
> *What difference does it make, brother?*
> *Give them all a fling!*

Chapter Fourteen

Terry had left the rooms just a little after Bill; just giving herself time to dress and makeup her face. Then, when walking through the casino she spotted Bill getting seated at the blackjack table. For a moment she almost walked over to him and then decided, reluctantly, that he didn't want to see her right then. Anyway, she reasoned, she had to go to the Golden Nugget and find Dave Baxter.

She got a cab outside of the hotel and then a few minutes later was in town, stepping into the Golden Nugget. She moved through the casino and finally found a spot where she could lookup at the small stage and watch the musicians play. Dave's group was on at the time she arrived, and she ordered a drink. It wasn't ten minutes later that they stepped off the stage one at a time as the men of the new group took over. Dave had spotted her from the stage and she'd motioned to him to come over when he was free. Now he stepped over to her side.

"Where's Bill?"

"Couldn't get him to come."

"I wondered if you could come out to the Sands tomorrow. Just happen to drop in."

"How will I know where to find you?" he asked,

sitting down beside her.

"We'll say that you saw me here tonight and I invited you up to see us. Maybe that might work. You can gab it up with Bill and maybe...Maybe talk him into blowing a bit with you."

"Okay, fine!"

A man stepped up to them and started talking to Dave. After a moment Baxter turned and said: "Sorry, gotta buzz off!"

She smiled and nodded. "See you tomorrow."

She stood and walked out of the casino and onto the street. For a moment she thought about gambling and then decided against it. Maybe back to the Sands and Bill would be in a more pleasant mood.

She sighed as she stepped into a cab and gave the driver the directions. She wondered how long it was going to last. How long Bill was going to continue to run. He couldn't do it forever, that much she knew, and she had the feeling that he knew it too.

Ten minutes later she was stepping through the casino of the Sands, looking for Bill. He wasn't at the black jack table nor at the roulette. Either at the bar or in their rooms. She decided that the best chance was to check the bar.

She stepped through the crowds and headed in the direction of the set of small tables around the large bar. It only took her a moment to spot Bill.

Then she jerked up as if slapped.

But that couldn't be him! she cried, inwardly. There was a woman with that man,

Then the man turned more in her direction and she recognized the features.

First fear cluttered through her brain, then a fluttering sensation clawed at Terry's stomach. Her whole body burned, and she felt a dizziness.

Confusion flashed through her. Confusion because of the reaction. Seeing Bill Carter with another woman. And from the way they were intimately holding hands she knew that it wasn't just a friendly conversation. And she couldn't help noticing the way the woman kept pushing her knee against his leg.

She felt sick, then. She'd given up everything for Bill Carter and now she realized what a complete waste it had been.

No, she thought, *she had probably known before, but hadn't been willing to admit it to herself.*

Before Laura had entered his life, Bill had always been one to play up to any board willing to go off with him. And now he was simply doing his old thing.

The scene before her hammered it into her conscious mind with such a powerful force that abruptly she found her legs weak and then her hands shaking.

The next reaction was anger. And slowly that built as she saw the woman lean closer to Bill and brush her lips on his cheek,

Then she saw red and the next thing she knew she was standing in front of the two startled people, insane fury firing from her eyes.

* * * * * * *

Bill looked up at Terry, recognizing her build, shape and form, but not immediately being able to make out her identity through the haze of liquor that

156

had managed to dull his brain and fuzz his vision. It took a moment to focus.

"Hell, hi there, Terry!" he shouted in a much too loud a voice.

Several people turned to look.

"Come on, Bill, let's go on up to the rooms!" Terry managed in a tight, controlled voice.

"Shell no!" he cried, reaching for her arm and pulling on it. But Terry jerked out of his grasp.

"Come on!" she demanded.

"Swell, look at shat!" he whispered to Sara, turning and looking at the other woman sitting next to him at the table.

There was a heavy silence as Terry glared at him and then she suddenly exploded. A hand slapped across Bill's face, stinging his brain momentarily sober.

He half stood, shocked by the blow. His mind cleared slightly and his eyes focused. He could see red hate in Terry's eyes. Her face was tensed with hard lines.

"You come along now!" she said in a low, hissing tone of voice. "Right now!"

He could see she was serious, but he didn't feel serious and suddenly it all seemed completely ridiculously silly, and for a moment it struck his drunken mind as being funny. First he felt the smile spread on his lips and then a bubbling laugh broke from them, but it was cut short when the back of Terry's hand slapped across the other side of his face. The impact of the blow turned his head and he felt himself flare violently, standing and raising a fist to swing at the girl.

But there was something that showed in her

eyes that stopped him for a split second and then his instincts took control of his muscles and he relaxed. But his tongue became immediately in action:

"Get the hell out!" he shouted, the fury raising his voice several notes higher. "We're finished!"

Terry half smiled as she announced: "You said a mouth full! I should have known I couldn't help you. You don't want help!" She had spoken the words so evenly and emotionless that Bill could only stare after her as she half ran away, a hand covering her lips. He watched her form move through the crowd and then disappear.

Slowly he slid down back into his chair and turned toward Sara who was looking at him with a mixture of shock and horror.

He tried to smile: "It's been coming for a while!"

Sara didn't say anything for a moment and then finally reached for her drink and gulped on it. "You ever tried that with me...*and I'd kill you!*"

"Come on, baby! Why should I do that? Terry's just a little tramp!"

Sara cringed at the words but didn't say anything. After a few moments she managed to relax her face muscles. Ten minutes later both of them seemed to have forgotten the whole thing. Finally she stood and smiled: "Let's get going!"

He didn't need any encouragement. Anything to get that sexual escape. More than ever now, because he had a sick feeling in his stomach and he didn't want to think about what might have caused it. It had begun when Terry had rushed out.

It only took them about ten minutes to get to Sara's room and then as she closed the door behind

158

them she turned and looked into his eyes. There was a mixture of mild anger and wild desire. She didn't have to say what her eyes were telling him: she didn't like what had happened in the cocktail lounge and would probably have pulled the sex rug out from under him except for one important fact: she liked his sexing! And she needed sex more than she needed self pride or anything else.

Her arms slipped around his neck and she pressed her body lightly against his. He could feel the warmth of her even through the dress.

His fingers worked on the zipper on the back of the gown and finally managed to draw it half way down. He felt the giggle first, before he heard it.

"What you trying to do? Undress me?" she asked, laughing and stepping back.

"What you shink?" he countered between clenched teeth. The desire and heat was already working his body into a desperate fit of need. He reached out for her and she stepped back from his hands.

"Take it easy! Give a girl a sec!" she told him letting the dress slide downwards to her waist. Then she unhooked her bra and swung out of it in one swift movement that freed her breasts.

A laugh welled in him and then he let his hands drop to her waist and half rip the dress from her body.

She gasped, startled.

"That dress cost money!" she complained. But her eyes were bright with excitement.

He pulled her against him, feeling the warmth of her even through his jacket and shirt.

But hardly had their lips touched than she

159

started working his jacket off him and then ripped the shirt aside. She moved her breasts against his chest, moaning in delight.

"Oh, you give me the tingles!" she almost hissed in his ear, biting the lobe between her teeth. It was almost like broad satire.

Her hips worked against his and the suggestive action was more than he could take under the strong effects of the liquor and her body. He all but pushed her toward the bed and she stumbled back, her waist and upper torso slamming onto the bed, with her legs dangling over the side.

He pulled off his pants and moved to her before she had a chance to change position. They didn't wait, but strained themselves together with such wild force and savage desperation that it was over much too fast to even begin to satisfy their now feverish bodies.

It had started again and he knew it wouldn't stop for a long time, and that's the way he wanted it. He didn't want to think of Terry; the escape he'd used to run away from the fact that he couldn't have Laura Jones again.

He dipped into the well that was Sara. This was the bottomless pit that he needed and would use to satisfy that need.

The well closed in around his awareness. He didn't think of time, and lost complete track of it along with conscious awareness.

* * * * * * *

Don Jenson looked in amazement at Terry. She had just walked into the club and seated herself at one of the dance floor tables. She was wearing a tight fitting red dress that showed every curve in her body. But the thing that most amazed him was the fact that she was alone.

At the intermission break he walked down and greeted her with an opening, bitter statement: "So you're back after the long weekend!"

"Don't, Don," she pleaded, offering him a seat.

"I'm sorry," he said, relaxing and sitting in the chair next to hers. "What's new?"

"It's finished," she told him. "Between Bill and myself."

Don nodded. "It was finished before you let it get started, but you were too blind. Bill doesn't care about anything. It might take him a month, a day, a week, or years to completely snap out of it."

"I know. I thought it might only be weeks but..." she sighed heavily. "Let's not talk about it!" she told him.

"I came here because it's the only place I know where to go. Think I can get the job back?" she asked, almost afraid that Hanson's fury would still be aimed at her.

Don smiled and reached out a hand, patting hers. "Sure! Why not? Hanson has simmered down. Every day he calls or stops in, hoping that Bill's returned. But..."

"You mean that he'd take Bill back, after what...?"

"That's about it. Maybe it might happen. Who knows?" Don commented, without much conviction in his voice. "But anyway, stop worrying. We could use a good female singer. How 'bout doing a set. Blow a few numbers tonight to warm up the voice?"

She smiled and gripped his hand. There was a tenderness in her eyes, and Don had the feeling that maybe at last he might have a chance with Terry, now that Bill was out of the picture. He knew that he could easily be urged to change his mind about making the point with a broad in the business. He took a breath and blurted out before he knew what was happening. "Doing anything, tonight, later?"

She gave him a knowing look and smiled, squeezing his fingers again, this time almost seductively. "You know, Don I think I like that idea of yours!"

Chapter Fifteen

When Bill awakened in the hotel rooms of Sara Cummings, alone, a dryness in his mouth and an ache in his head, he had the feeling of something missing. For a while he couldn't figure out what it was; he couldn't remember what it could be.

Then it crashed in on him.

Terry had left him!

It wasn't the statement that she had left him that was so startling, but rather the effect it had on his mind.

He sat there in bed, numbly looking across the room, trying to remember how it had happened but he couldn't get the details focused in his brain. The only reason that he could think of and remember was that Terry had seen him with Sara

He thought back. For the first time letting his mental eye look long and hard upon Laura Jones, the girl he was going to marry, and who was dead.

Nausea swept through him and he felt that horrible clawing at his gut. Slowly he slid out of bed and moved to the dresser where there was a bottle of whiskey. He reached for it and then his hand paused in midair, freezing.

Another bender? his mind asked.

Where would that lead? Death, given time. If he had any real guts he'd find a gun and stick it in his mouth and blow it like a trumpet to hell and back.

That's not what Laura would want. She always said to live in the now, not the past or the future. "Now is all you have" was one of her favorite lines.

Now was nothing, just hell and crap and nothing at all.

Terry had left him. His career was shot. All he had to look forward to was more booze and women like Sara to dive into.

Laura would be disgusted with him!

But he didn't want to think about Laura and her dear, lovable body that had been given to him and him alone. He didn't want to be aware of the fact that he could never possess it again; hold her to him. He didn't want that sharp pain to dig through him every time she came before his mind.

And the boozing helped!

Yet his hand wouldn't go to the bottle, yet. It kept frozen in the air.

Think about Terry and her ripe, throbbing body, lustful but in love with him. Her eyes dark and bright; her brimming breasts that rose and fell eagerly to his touch. Think about Terry Anson and her freely giving love. Her caring, tenderness, understanding beyond logic. Think about this woman who was alive, throbbing with passion, with a living hunger.

She was alive and now. And in love with him.

The word love stopped him.

She had been his now, and he'd blow her away.

The bottle had abruptly come up to his mouth. He couldn't think of Terry anymore, because that was finished and gone as dead as Laura was for him! And that thought gulped raw whiskey down his throat, numbing into his stomach. He swallowed hard again, anxiously and eagerly, waiting for the soothing effects.

What was left to him now, outside of a bottle to suckle?

Think about Sara and her never ending demands for a man's body against her; the driving power of her form that wouldn't stop working until the man was unable to respond. Her needs were unlimited. Think of Sara and her coarse love making—desiring and forcing. Wanting the hurt and brutal force of sex to drive through her.

The whiskey took slight effect, and he swallowed more. He wondered where Sara was. He could use her right then. It wasn't nice of her to leave him alone. Not like this, when he was crying inwardly because he couldn't have the escape that was in the form of Terry Anson.

There that woman's name was, again.

Terry Anson!

She was another he didn't want to think about. He forced himself to break off that thought. There was an unsettling feeling and emotion that rushed through him as he thought of the woman.

He laughed inwardly at himself for having been a fool in judging people. He'd thought of Terry as being nothing but a little slutting whore. But that had been all wrong. Sure, she would let herself find lovers. Yet hadn't he picked up his share of women in the past? What made him think that society's "double standard" had anything to do with real moral issues. If it was sinful for her to let a man into

165

her pants, it was just as sinful for the man that got into them. She had the same right as any other human being. And you didn't judge a man by how he was in the rack, but rather what he was as a person. What he could and did do for others. And what had Terry done? Given not only her body to him, but also all her self pride and her career. The career could be gained back, if she crawled long enough. But the pride, that was something different. She might fool herself, rationalizing but...

She'd sold out for him, and all that he'd given her was dirt. Slapped her verbally in the face every chance he got. He snapped his fingers and she did as all slaves will do for their masters. Anything he desired.

And he knew why she had left him. It had finally been too much for her; seeing him openly with Sara Cummings.

He took another strong drink and then another. The room around him was beginning to spin, now. Just as he was about to swallow some more whiskey the door opened and Sara glided in.

Her eyes moved pointedly to his body which was completely nude and free for her to examine.

"My, my I see you are awake and...alive!" Her eyes made the last word suggestive. "How long?"

"Just a few minutes!" he said, gazing at the bulge of her breast where they pushed out the blouse.

"Get undressed!" he commanded, without any thought as to what she might desire. It didn't matter to him. He had to escape from his thoughts. He had to run from Terry, now, too. In fact, he realized, he had to run from her more than anybody in the living

166

world. And it was only in Sara's body that he would have that escape.

"Come on...hurry!" he told her, stepping toward her.

"Maybe I don't want to!" She broke off, because her eyes were already beginning to give her away. She wanted it and bad. Her face flushed and then suddenly with such desperate speed that he couldn't really follow her actions, she undressed. First ripping at the blouse. Then her skirt. Bra flew across the room and then her pink panties followed it. She rushed into his arms, already her breath coming in panting gasps.

Her tongue surged into his mouth, working rhythmically with the squirming action of her hips. Then she moved from him and a moment later they were on the bed, totally devouring one another. But even as they were convulsing to the peak of ecstasy, he couldn't get the idea out of his drunk dazed mind that it should be Terry's body working against his, not this little showbiz nympho.

And that thought startled him so violently that he forced himself onto Sara again, working her body and then finally escaping from all awareness in the eager heat of their sexual embraces.

He was already beginning to forget Laura!

How long it was he didn't know. But when he awoke he was again alone, but also with a bitter taste of a terrible awareness in his throat.

Terry!

He needed her.

He wanted her.

And what was worst of all was the fact that he realized that he loved her.

When the change had taken place he didn't really know or why it had. The only logical conclusion he could come up with was that she had been there when he needed her, silent and understanding when there wasn't really any room for understanding.

She had waited until he had pushed her too far.

He slid out of bed and got dressed, then walked from the room and down the hall toward his own. There was only one thing left to do. It had been bad enough without Laura; that had been overwhelming. And in his self pity he had managed to completely destroy his life completely. There was nothing left. Nothing that counted; nothing that mattered. And he knew that the slow death wouldn't come fast enough. The bottle death took too much time and energy. And vaguely he was suddenly aware that a woman's body didn't offer the kind of escape he needed. Not just a woman's body like Sara. Too late he had realized exactly what Terry had grown to mean to him and now there wasn't anything left to do but seek the quick, easy way.

A gun? Gas? Sleeping pills?

Maybe the latter. That was a nice way to go out; quiet and easy. Complete escape. Utter end. Nothing left for the next morning when you have to face yourself drunkenly in the mirror, your head throbbing with pains and your whole body in a tight vise. The mirror told too damned much. It spoke soundlessly to a man.

He stepped into the bathroom and looked at his face in the mirror and was a little shocked at what he saw.

Bearded and older seeming. His hair too long,

unkempt. Deep circles under his eyes and lines creasing his bloated features.

Booze face!

It wasn't the face that Laura had fallen in love with. Not the handsome, clean cut features topped with curly hair.

Laura's face appeared in the reflection. She smiled first and then frowned:

"Is this the solution?" she asked, a tear running down her cheek. "Is that what I brought you to?"

Her face slowly faded and then Terry's took shape. She, too, was sad-eyed, and then she flared angrily:

"Well, it's just what you deserve. After you made a little whore out of me. That's what you did! You used my body but not the love I wanted to give you!"

Don was next. Don Jenson, buddy, fellow "rack the girls up in bed." He frowned and looked grim and serious:

"Look, Bill, how long are you going to let this work on you? You can kill yourself; that would take more guts than you have! So you'll drink yourself to death?"

Then a face blended over that man's. He recognized it as his own but the way it had been before Laura had died.

"There you are, sucker. Let a woman in your life and she'll twist it apart. But I tried to warn you...you won't ever listen. So, now all the dreams, the wanting to say something with your music, are all gone. Just because of a broad!"

"Shut up!" he yelled at the face.

It smiled at him:

169

"Good! Get mad. That means you have some fight in you, yet. You could still maybe pick up the pieces or start new. Why not give it a spin. You know that's what Laura would have wanted!"

"Shut up!" he screamed at his reflection, turning and moving from the bathroom. A few minutes later he was standing before a roulette table, down in the casino, staring numbly at the little ball that went round and round, jumping gaily from one number to another, not caring what might really happen, or where it might land. Carefree. Like he'd been.

He thought about death and then decided.

He was a gambling man. He had something like $2,000 in his wallet. He'd blow it on red and if it won, he'd face life. If it lost, he'd just ended it.

Leave it to lady luck!

He dropped the bills on the red and the people around him at the table glanced in surprise, but said nothing.

The ball went round and round, spinning, dropping, bouncing, dropping and then sliding over three numbers.

Red!

He'd won. A thrill rushed through him. He'd won. Then he stood surprised. He had wanted to live. He realized suddenly that he wanted to live; something that he really hadn't known before. And he knew something else: that even if the Black had come up he couldn't have killed himself. It was all a game, a fantastic game that he was creating in his brain.

Then he saw the broader game.

The game of life he was playing for the mere drama of it. He never had planned on letting himself fall too deep. He had never planned on going down the drain completely. Just suffer a little, find himself and then deal with what was left.

He stood there, looking at the dealer as he pushed another $4,000 toward him. He started. "I only had two Gs down."

"You won, stood, and red came up again!" the man explained automatically.

Bill scooped up the $8,000, stuffing his pockets full and rushing toward the bar. He needed a drink to celebrate. Celebrate finding himself.

He paused ten feet from the bar, breathing hard.

Suddenly he realized that he didn't want a drink. He didn't need one, really. The idea made him slightly sick.

"Say, Bill Carter!" a voice called out to him, and he turned to look. For a moment he couldn't place the face, and then he recognized the features. Dave Baxter.

"What you doing here, in town?" he cried to the sax man, suddenly glad to see somebody that he knew that wasn't female.

"Working a gig...saw Terry the other evening, but I hear she left a day ago."

Bill nodded.

"Well, how are things?" he asked, shaking Baxter's hand. "Let's me buy you a drink!"

"Sure thing!"

They sat at the bar and ordered, but when Bill had received the highball he'd ordered he couldn't even sip it.

"What's wrong?" Baxter asked.

"Been on a lost weekend. No more booze now though!"

They talked for a long time. Dave suggested that he come up into town and see their act. "Blow a few with us."

The thought of playing suddenly excited him, and he knew that it was time to stop running to stop escaping from the fact that Laura Jones was dead.

* * * * * * *

He had spent three sober days in Vegas and still had a little over $5,000 safely tucked away. Each night and each set he'd sat in with Dave Baxter, the man seemed to sense that this was what he needed.

The time had given him a chance to think things out.

Laura was dead. He could face that almost unemotionally. And the time…faded the horrid nightmare blues he'd been playing for his dearly beloved Laura. Maybe that had been his mourning period.

He was of the living and he had to live with the living. He could still hold Laura dear in his heart; but buried like she belonged. Instead of having felt so sorry for himself he would, in time, be able to look upon the times with Laura as something wonderful, and something that had taught and given to him so much. What if he'd never met her? He wouldn't have known what it was to love. He would never have known real love and what it meant, and how important it could be in a man's life. There was more than just bumming around, blowing a horn, mindlessly going from day to day. Love added a dimension to life that was totally new and richly fulfilling. And the fact was, hard as that might be to swallow down, that one could fall in love with many people. The trick was to focus on one and make it work.

He'd had a wonderful real love affair; and Laura and taught him something very special that he'd never forget.

When he got back to where the group was blowing maybe it would be possible to pick some of the shattered pieces of his life and career and start over, fresh. That was the thing he had to face next. Maybe Hanson had cooled off. But the most important thing was Terry. Would she take him back? Chances were he'd blown that. He realized that she had given him a lot and he had merely taken. He wanted her back. He wanted to give a little of the debt back to that woman who had sold herself to a guy who didn't want her or help from anybody.

Now he wanted help. He wanted to get back on track with his own group, if that was possible.

On impulse he put a phone call to Don, hoping to find out how things stood. The man was delighted to hear from him.

"You sound great!" Don announced, after the opening exchange.

"How would you know?"

"A little birdie told us. Actually, Dave told Terry all about how you were blowing great, and how you'd—"

"You're kidding!" Bill exploded, surprised, delighted, but somewhat confused and unnerved.

Before he could say anything, Don said: "Here, Bill, somebody wants to speak to you."

"Wait!" Bill cried, wanting to find out more. But a moment later a woman's voice came over the receiver.

"Hi," Terry greeted warmly, "you're coming home? At last?"

"I'm coming home!" was his reply.

"I'll be waiting for you," Terry assured him.

* * * * * * *

The night air of the club was filled with smoke. The small combo on the stand was just finishing a number. Finally it came to an end and the leader stepped up to the mike. He fingered the trumpet nervously for a moment and then said:

"Ladies and Gents, since we've been back together, now for six months, a lot has happened. We just recorded an album...and things look busting. One of the songs was named after a woman that means a lot to all of us, not only for her talent, but also for her personal help. Then so on with the show. Here's Terry Anson to sing an original song written by our bass guy, Don, by the name of, strangely enough, 'Terry'!"

The man stepped back and Terry bounced up to the stage. Before she nodded to the man she said:

"Only one thing more, the guy that wrote the lyrics is named Bill Carter!" she smiled, knowingly.

Terry nodded and then started singing. But deep inside her heart was more than singing. The group was together again, and on its way.

And from the looks of things, her name would soon be Mrs. Bill Carter, wife of a very, very famous trumpet player!

About the Author

Charles Nuetzel was born in San Francisco in 1934, and writes:

"As long as I can remember I wanted to be a writer. It was a dream I never thought would materialize. But with the help of Forrest J Ackerman, who became my agent, I managed to finally make it into print.

"I was lucky enough not only in selling my work to publishers but also ending up packaging books for some of them, and finally becoming a 'publisher' much like those who had bought my first novels. From there it as a simple leap to editing not only a science-fiction anthology, but also a line of SF books for Powell Sci-Fi back in the 1960s. Throughout these active professional years I had the chance to design some covers and do graphic cover layouts for pocket books & magazines."

Much of his work in covers and graphics are a result of having had a father who was a professional commercial artist, and who did a number of covers for sci-fi magazines in the 1950s and later for pocket books—even for some of Mr. Nuetzel's books.

In retirement he has become involved in swing dancing, a long time lover of Big Band jazz. But more interestingly world travels have taken him (and his wife Brigitte) across the world, to Hawaii, Caribbean, Mexico, Kenya, Egypt, Peru, having a lifelong interest in ancient civilizations. His website is full of thousands of pictures taken during these trips.